CRASH COURSE . . .

Harry Ackors paced up and down in his big house on Alder Street. From the information he had from the test shot today at the Labs, they had perfected the weapon, even though the ecologists had waded in and bungled things grandly.

His own shadow crossed the room in front of him, and it brought a sudden sweat to his brow. His shadow agent. If he failed in this mission, or became captured or compromised, the shadow agent would move in and eliminate him in minutes. That way Ackors would not be an embarrassment to the mother country. But he hadn't failed totally. He had slowed the project down over the past three years, and that had been his job. Now the program was nearly complete. What he needed now was a bold move, a counterstroke they wouldn't anticipate. That might be enough to save him. It would have to be extreme, brilliant, effective. . . .

By morning Ackors had his plan. He and Willy worked carefully setting it up. At last they had it ready, a pick-up loaded with 40 cases of 60-percent dynamite. The entire front bumper was rigged as an impact detonator. With the switch off, the bumper could be used to ram into things, but with it on, it acted as a detonator for the whole load. The plan was for Willy to drive to the lab grounds, get through the guards, tie down the steering wheel, and aim the pick-up at Building 176, then jump. When he hit, Willy would run like hell. . . .

THE PENETRATOR SERIES:

#1 THE TARGET IS H
#2 BLOOD ON THE STRIP
#3 CAPITOL HELL
#4 HIJACKING MANHATTAN
#5 MARDI GRAS MASSACRE
#6 TOKYO PURPLE
#7 BAJA BANDIDOS
#8 THE NORTHWEST CONTRACT
#9 DODGE CITY BOMBERS
#10 THE HELLBOMB FLIGHT
#11 TERROR IN TAOS
#12 BLOODY BOSTON
#13 DIXIE DEATH SQUAD
#14 MANKILL SPORT
#15 THE QUEBEC CONNECTION
#16 DEEPSEA SHOOTOUT
#17 DEMENTED EMPIRE
#18 COUNTDOWN TO TERROR
#19 PANAMA POWER PLAY
#20 THE RADIATION HIT
#21 THE SUPERGUN MISSION
#22 HIGH DISASTER
#23 DIVINE DEATH
#24 CRYOGENIC NIGHTMARE
#25 FLOATING DEATH
#26 MEXICAN BROWN
#27 THE ANIMAL GAME
#28 THE SKYHIGH BETRAYERS
#29 ARYAN ONSLAUGHT
#30 COMPUTER KILL
#31 OKLAHOMA FIREFIGHT
#32 SHOWBIZ WIPEOUT
#33 SATELLITE SLAUGHTER
#34 DEATH RAY TERROR

WRITE FOR OUR FREE CATALOG

If there is a Pinnacle Book you want—and you cannot find it locally—it is available from us simply by sending the title and price plus 50¢ per order and 10¢ per copy to cover mailing and handling costs to:

Pinnacle Book Services
P.O. Box 690
New York, N.Y. 10019

Please allow 4 weeks for delivery. New York State and California residents add applicable sales tax.

___Check here if you want to receive our catalog regularly.

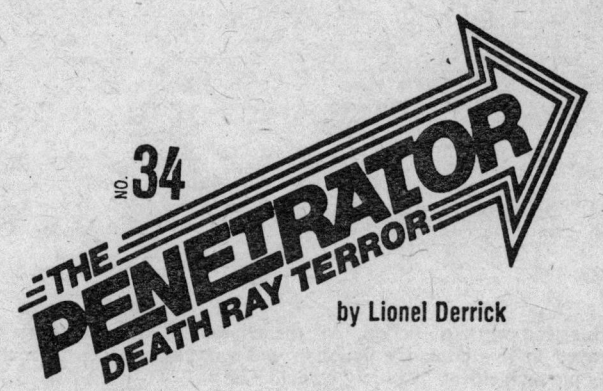

by Lionel Derrick

PINNACLE BOOKS   LOS ANGELES

This is a work of fiction. All the characters and events portrayed in this book are fictional, and any resemblance to real people or incidents is purely coincidental.

PENETRATOR #34: DEATH RAY TERROR

Copyright © 1979 by Pinnacle Books

All rights reserved, including the right to reproduce this book or portions thereof in any form.

An original Pinnacle Books edition, published for the first time anywhere.

Special acknowledgments to Chet Cunningham

First printing, December 1979

ISBN: 0-523-40631-2

Cover illustration by George Wilson

Printed in the United States of America

PINNACLE BOOKS, INC.
2029 Century Park East
Los Angeles, California 90067

PROLOGUE

Duty is loyalty, love and understanding,
   Melded into a perfect union by a great need;
Heightened and crystalized by emotion;
   Launched with pragmatic realism
By the gentle, the compassionate, the strong of heart.
                             —Heather Ambrose

Joanna Tabler stood at the window of her thirty-second-floor office and stared unseeing across the big city. Today the skyline of New York did not stir her; the hazy, smoggy air only gave her a headache, and she wished desperately that Mark Hardin were there with her. How long had it been since she had seen him? She couldn't remember. Too damn long, that was for sure.

She walked around the plush interior of the big corner office, trying to get up some enthusiasm for her assignment. She was on the track of some far-out ecology nut who thought she was the successor to the Weathermen and was not only talking ecology but knocking heads and blowing up buildings and small dams and fighting any "progress" that she thought violated and raped the land. Great, big deal. A dandy job for a Justice Department agent.

Joanna pushed the button on her desk and asked

Martha to bring in a cup of coffee. She took it from the woman, who was in her fifties and had the appearance of a gentle grandmother, but who was a J-4 agent in her own right and the best pistol shot among the female agents in the New York area.

"Thanks, Martha. I'm in a mood today."

The older woman smiled and left without a word. She knew the feeling.

"Dammit, Mark, where are you?" Joanna said out loud. She sipped the coffee and stared at the Hudson River. She'd first met Mark Hardin when she had her gun at his back inside a taxi and she was trying to get some information from him.

Since then she had discovered that he was a one-man army, a powerful justice force in his own right, working inside or outside the law to rid the land of as many criminals and mobsters as he could.

Joanna knew the whole story. It began when Mark had been discharged from the army after Vietnam, not entirely healed in body or spirit, and gone to a friend of a friend's mountain retreat in the Calico mountains outside Barstow, California. There he mended and became a friend of an ancient Cheyenne medicine chief, David Red Eagle, who recognized Mark's Indian heritage.

Mark had been orphaned at an early age and had lived in a succession of foster homes as he grew up, and he had lost most information about his parents.

The Stronghold had been built in the desert by Dr. Willard Haskins, a retired professor from USC who constructed his retreat in the upper areas of an old borax mine. Professor Haskins's niece, Donna, was there, and she and Mark fell in love. As Mark and Donna tried to discover his roots in the Los Angeles public records, the Mafia thought they were digging up information on one of their crooked deals and ordered both young people eliminated.

Donna died in a fiery car crash, and Mark launched a campaign to avenge her death and to rid the nation of as many criminals and hoodlums as he could. The Professor and David Red Eagle formed his back-up team, his home base, and his intelligence section.

Now, after more than 30 campaigns against the enemy, Mark was still going strong, and Joanna wondered where he was. She could not call the Stronghold and talk to him. Phone calls were too easy to trace. She hated to write letters, so for months at a time she and Mark lost track of each other.

She remembered the times when he had helped her—in fact, saved her life several times. They had also worked together on some cases, in spite of his objections.

Joanna sat on the couch and stared out at the city. She was 28 years old, a native of Washington, D.C., and a J-6-class agent with the Justice Department. Her office was a cover, the Diogenes Investigations firm. They took no civilian cases, were not listed in the phone book, and brushed aside any attempts to engage them on a job.

Joanna's platinum blond hair was short again, and beautifully set. She had been a model for a while and showed that training in her excellent use of make-up and taste in clothes. Her hazel eyes were troubled now, giving her expression a touch of wistfulness as she thought of Mark.

Sometimes she didn't see how he kept going. He had been shot and stabbed and broken so many times, she had lost count. He had fought crime in

Japan, France, Mexico, and Central America—over half the world—and still he came back for more. He was a miracle man. In his escapades, however he had irritated the law and was now on the "Most Wanted" lists of the FBI and dozens of police agencies. The FBI had a special man assigned to search for Mark, who was known as the Penetrator.

She had met him through her work for the Justice Department, and her boss, Dan Griggs, knew Mark, too, and did his part in a gentle cover-up to keep Mark's identity hidden.

Only these five—David Red Eagle, the Professor, Dan Griggs, Joanna, and a sheriff's captain in Los Angeles—knew for sure who Mark was and where he could be found. His life was in their hands. But they never wavered.

Now Joanna Tabler sighed, walked back to her desk, and settled down, reading a folder Dan had given her on her latest target.

Chapter 1

YOU'LL HAVE A BLAST

Claude Young slumped in his pick-up in the parking lot at the Los Alamos Scientific Laboratories near Los Alamos, New Mexico, and looked at his watch again. His left arm came up slowly, his eyes took a moment to focus, and then he read the digital numbers on his watch. Fifteen minutes yet. The man said nine o'clock A.M., so he had to wait. Claude wasn't sure why. The man had told him to wait, and that was reason enough. Oh, the man didn't pay him or anything like that. It wasn't a job he had to do, the way he had a job to do here at the Labs. He didn't do this so he could get paid for it. But he had to do it. Claude tried to think exactly why.

He remembered the man had told him to. They had talked a lot of times, and sometimes the man helped him work on his pick-up. Usually they played a game with a swinging watch that made Claude sleepy. The man could make him go to sleep in the middle of the day. He didn't remember much about the games now.

But the man said he should sit in his pick-up in the parking lot this morning after work until nine o'clock, so he was still there. His shift ended at 8:30—the night shift, maintenance. Usually he would be home by now.

His mother would worry about him. Claude was never late. It was nice of the man here at the Labs to give him the job. Not that it was the best work, but most people wouldn't hire him to do anything. He didn't like people who called him dumb. He stared out the truck window and waved at one of the men he knew who worked there.

"Hi there, Claude. I thought you'd be home by now. There's some good TV on this morning."

"Yeah, Mr. Miller. I'll be go . . . go . . . going home soon."

Miller grinned and walked on by.

Claude felt better. See, see! That man didn't tease him or say he was dumb, or call him a damned M.R. The thought brought a glow of warmth and satisfaction to Claude. Still he sat there. The numbers on his digital watch changed slowly until it read exactly nine o'clock A.M. and triggered the wrist alarm.

Claude heard it and blinked. He automatically started the pick-up. His eyes were alert now. He checked for traffic, then drove out of the parking spot. His movements were slow, studied, certain. He knew exactly what he had to do. Claude went to the last row of the big parking lot, then turned left toward the gate restricting all but official cars from driving inside the lab grounds themselves. His eyes fixed ahead on the gate. There was no barrier, just a guard with a clipboard to log in and out the official vehicles.

Claude saw the guard hold up his clipboard and wave. That was when Claude pushed down on the gas pedal. The 1973 blue Chevy pick-up jumped forward, the guard yelled and spun away out of the path of the left bumper, and the pick-up shot through the gate into the restricted zone. Claude didn't look back. He drove two blocks, turned left, then stared ahead at the next security gate. The buzzer alarm on his wrist kept sounding, but Claude didn't hear it. He was not smiling. His face had a slight frown as if he were remembering, concentrating on his instructions so he would do them exactly right. If he did, the man said he would buy him a brand-new pick-up, one with four-wheel drive and either a big six-cylinder engine of a diesel, whichever he wanted!

As Claude rolled up to the next gate, he could see that it had been swung closed. It was a metal affair made of inch piping and wire. It was a cattle gate, not really for security. He slowed and saw the guard take his hand away from the .45 automatic on his hip and look down at his clipboard. That's when Claude floor-boarded the pick-up, and the well-tuned V-8 engine wound up, jolting the blue rig forward. Before the guard saw what was happening, and too quickly for him to reach for his weapon, the pick-up grazed him on the side, cartwheeling him beyond the guard post. The truck slammed into the security gate, ripped it free from the hinge end, and dragged it half a block down the road before it fell away.

Claude didn't look back. The buzzer on his wrist kept sounding. It would continue until he turned it off. Driving carefully now, Claude counted one building, two, then three. At the fourth one, he turned into the driveway and went around to the back. It was Building 214, but Claude didn't realize that. Now all he had to do was back up the rig and bump it into the building right beside the rear steps, just as the man had told him to do. He didn't have to go too fast, 15 miles an hour would be enough. That would dent Little Pearl, his pick-up, but the man said he would buy Claude a brand-new one! Claude saw a guard run around the far end of the building with his .45 pistol out, but Claude didn't have time to stop and talk with him. He put the rig into reverse and jammed down on the gas pedal.

The pick-up roared backward. The innocuous-looking box hanging on the rear bumper had been attached only a half-hour before. Claude didn't know it was there. Extending outward 6 inches at three places on the wooden box were pencil-sized steel rods. As the blue pick-up smashed into the wooden siding of Building 214, the steel rod on the near corner plunged inward, activated the detonator, and 30 quarter-pound bricks of C-4 plastique explosive went off with a belching, gut sucking, shattering roar.

The near wall of the wooden building blasted inward. The metal box of the pick-up directed much of the energy toward the building, before the massive explosive power instantly vaporized the rear half of the small truck, blasted the cab apart, and flung it 40 feet away like a split pea pod, cremating Claude Young where he sat. The crumpled, shattered front half of the cab melted from the intense heat, and everything that was flammable burned in a tenth of a second. Only the front tires remained recognizable as they burned intensely with thick, black smoke.

The explosion ignited the matchstick rubble of the back wall, which now burned fiercely, fueled by an erupted natural-gas pipeline. After the rear wall blew inward on the 40-foot-long, one-story frame building, two interior load-bearing walls collapsed, and the roof sagged, hesitated, then went crashing down in a white rain of plaster dust, splintering boards, and asphalt shingles.

It took Wilbur Winslow four minutes and ten seconds to get to Building 214 after the explosion. He had been less than half a mile away when he heard it. He had just been alerted that "Crazy Claude" had crashed both guard gates. Winslow, as head of security, wasn't too concerned about Claude. He knew the boy, and even though he was a little slow, he definitely was not dangerous.

"What the hell?" Winslow growled as he skidded to a stop in the driveway, far enough from the flames of Building 214 to be safe. Winslow was tall, willow-thin, and from Texas. He'd been in the Air Force for 26 years and couldn't give up wearing a uniform of some kind. He unwound himself from his cost-efficient Ford Fiesta and stared at the destruction. It looked like the goddamn war.

"My God in heaven!" he said softly. The cab of a pick-up, or what was left of it, was jammed against the building opposite 214. It was twisted into a nightmarish shape of burned upholstery and melted, agonized metal.

There was little left standing of Building 214. The far end was still upright. The back wall was gone, and a door swung haphazardly on one hinge. The dust hadn't even settled.

A guard ran up, his army-issue .45 still in his hand. His eyes were vacant, staring. His hands, arms, and face looked as if he had a massive sunburn. Small white bubbles covered his cheeks and forehead. He didn't seem able to talk, and wouldn't respond to Winslow's questions.

Wilbur gently took the .45 from the guard's hand and helped him lie down on the grass. He used his radio and called the ambulance. They said the fire department truck was already on the way. If the doctor were on the base, he would be contacted. Winslow headed toward the end of the building not burning. How many people had been inside when it blew?

He stepped up to a window and stared through, then picked off the remains of the glass and began to climb in.

"There's no point in going inside, Wilbur."

The security chief turned. The general director of the Los Alamos Scientific Laboratories, Dr. William Dessel, was a dozen feet behind him, one of his famous clipboards in his right hand.

"Looking for casualties," Winslow said.

"No one was working in this building today," Dr. Dessel countered. "It simply wasn't scheduled for use today, so there won't be any casualties inside. I suggest you get your man to the infirmary."

The fire engine whined to a stop. Four hoses were hooked up, as the labs' own fire department went to work on the blaze. The gas line was closed off at the nearest valve, and the firemen brought the flames under control in 15 minutes.

The ambulance arrived and took the burned guard away. He still hadn't talked and was in deep shock.

When the fire was beaten down, Winslow looked at his boss.

"You don't want me to go in there?" Winslow asked.

"No, Wilbur, I don't. You have no need to know, and this is strictly a top-secret, need-to-know project. You understand about our security. Unless someone were taking a nap in there, there was no one inside."

"Would you take a quick look, sir, or come with me?" Winslow asked.

At last Dr. Dessel nodded, and together they checked what they could of the building. They returned to Winslow's car a few minutes later.

"Who was the pick-up driver?" Dessel asked.

"Claude Young. A kid about nineteen. He's the slightly mentally retarded boy you hired about a year ago. He's never done anything out of line before."

"Until now, when he blows up a building, obliterates his first love, that blue pick-up, and in the process he is vaporized in the bomb's fireball."

"I'll check on him, sir. See what I can find out, who he's been associated with, what visitors he's had. His mother usually keeps close track of him."

Dr. Dessel frowned. "This is one time she should have kept a tighter rein."

"Not much left to see, I'm afraid," the director said. He didn't especially like dealing with people from the FBI, but this one seemed pleasant enough. He had phoned a report in right after the blast, and the FBI had been alerted and they'd sent Pete Sanchez over from their Santa Fe office. Now it was four o'clock P.M., and the FBI had landed.

Pete Sanchez looked at the building and made a quick tour of the blast site and what was left of the pick-up. There wasn't even the smell of burned flesh in the twisted cab. As he rode back to the office building with Dr. Dessel, he asked, "There was no one in the building at the time?"

"No," the doctor replied.

"And the only fatality was the driver, this Claude Young, a borderline mentally retarded employee?"

"Yes. I've known his parents for years. He's never broken even a minor rule here before. It seemed like a good job for him.

"I'm sure it was. From what you said on the phone, he would not have the slightest idea how to put together a bomb like the one that exploded here."

"That's true. Claude could do simple jobs, repetitive things, maintenance, janitorial. But nothing that took any initiative or reasoning power. This was simply beyond his capacity."

"And you've notified his parents?"

"Yes."

"I'd like to talk to the two guards manning the gates he went through, and the man in the hospital, if that's all right."

"I'll have the first two brought to your office."

Sanchez spent an hour with each guard, going over and over exactly what happened. Each man told his story, and before long Sanchez had the picture as well as they could reconstruct it. They couldn't tell if Young had been drunk, on some kind of dope, or simply his usual self when he tore through the gates. The guard in the hospital was still on the critical list and couldn't be questioned.

Sanchez talked to Dr. Dessel again just before seven o'clock that evening.

"As near as I can tell, Dr. Dessel, Claude worked his normal shift, finished at 8:30, and went to the parking lot, where he sat in the pick-up until about nine o'clock. Then he started his rig and drove to the first gate. There, he slowed as if he were going to stop, but gunned on through. At the second gate, he smashed through the metal security gate and hit the guard in the process but didn't injure him seriously. He says he'll be sore and stiff for a few days but he's okay. Once past the second guard, Claude drove to the rear of Building 214, backed into it, and detonated the powerful bomb.

"We haven't located any of the mechanisms or detonator from the bomb and probably won't. It was such an intense blast that the plastic parts, and even the metal parts, disintegrated, melted, or were vaporized. We're not sure what type of explosive until we run some lab tests, but my guess is plastique. My conclusions are that the boy could not have acted alone, that someone used him and let him die in the process, knowing full well that he would."

Dr. Dessel laid down the pencil with which he had been fashioning an endless chain of small circles.

"That's why they mounted the bomb on the rear bumper, so Claude could crash the gate and not set off the bomb there?"

"Yes. My guess is that he came to work as usual, and someone else during the morning, perhaps during the shift change, came in and mounted the box on the bumper. There could have been some pre-drilled holes or mounting brackets already put on the truck so the attachment could have been done in seconds with some type of metal lever snaps or come-alongs. Since the parking lot is outside the Lab security fence, anyone could have driven in during the morning rush and attached the bomb, then driven away."

"Any other security arrangement would be too cumbersome . . ." Dessel began.

"Dr. Dessel, I'm not criticizing your operation."

Sanchez paused. "I'm just trying to find out who and why. It would be a great help to know why that building was the target. I'll need it for my report as well. What special work was going on there?"

Dr. Dessel narrowed deep-set eyes and rubbed one hand across his face. "All I can tell you is that the building was being used occasionally for highly classified weapons research. In fact, we have six different buildings designated for work on this project. For increased security, we move the operation around at random times among the buildings. The code name is LONG REACH. You can use that in your report, and it will gain top-level attention. In this matter, I have a much higher restrictive clearance than you do, Mr. Sanchez, and I must maintain project security. What I've told you is plenty for your report."

Pete Sanchez looked up quickly. "Dr. Dessel, usually we get total cooperation from government facilities. However, you are correct. The title of the operation and the code name LONG REACH should be enough to alert our people to its importance."

He stood and snapped his thin briefcase shut. "I'll be around tomorrow morning, then I should be finished here. I want to talk to that burned guard if I can. Is there anything more that the department can do for you?"

"Yes, find out who is behind all of this."

"My job is just to investigate and report. Anything else will have to come from our main office. You might ask your high-level contacts to get in touch with our director."

"Yes, I may have to do that. I'm sorry, but this whole thing has me on edge. I can't figure out how anyone on the outside knew about our work here, let alone knew exactly which building to hit. Of course, they were one day late, but even so, that means someone knows far, far too much. Actually, it may be a blessing under the gravy. They destroyed nothing on the project, yet tipped their hand. Now at least we know someone out there is interested in stopping our work."

"I'll check out before I go tomorrow," Sanchez said.

Dr. Dessel watched Sanchez leave. He sat at his desk, making interlocking green and red circles on his pad, not even wondering what a psychologist would have to say in evaluating his doodling. The enemy had certainly made his intentions clear. Now Dessel was positive someone was sabotaging the project. This should bring some action from the outside. Probably not the FBI. Maybe the CIA? No, they were supposed to work only outside the United States.

He rubbed his forehead. The twinges of the migraine were coming back. They had begun when LONG REACH first started developing. Tonight's head-banger would be a beauty. He looked at his desk, put the papers, notices, and correspondence into two piles, then settled down with the last progress report on LONG REACH. He was fascinated by this program, and it was all he could do to keep his hands off it. But this overt strike by an enemy meant he had to accelerate the program as fast as he could. And security must be beefed up. He had the budget to double the guards, and he decided that he would. Dr. Dessel would give his superiors 24 hours to take some sort of definitive action to try to track down the enemy agents, and if they did nothing, then he would request action. He nodded. Yes, by God, this was too important a project to let some rum-nosed, three-martini-lunch bureaucrat foul up!

Chapter 2

ONE QUICK, EASY MURDER

Harry Ackors sat in his Buick Skylark on a slight rise where he could look down on the sprawling facility known as the Los Alamos Scientific Laboratories. He munched on a chocolate bar and sipped from a can of beer kept cold in its own insulated container. Wait. That was all he could do right now. But he was good at that, one of the best.

Ackors levered his 210 pounds from the seat and slid from the car. His watch showed it was 8:58 A.M. It should happen shortly, if it were going to.

He lifted 8 x 50 binoculars to his eyes and scanned the Labs, but he was too far away to see much. Ackors dropped the glasses on the cord around his neck and wiped a trail of sweat from his forehead. Every summer he realized that he should lose some weight. But it was a pain in the ass to try. He was five-foot-eight and 210 pounds. So it was a little too much. He got his work done.

Ackors brought the glasses up again and searched the Labs but could find little to interest him. Sweat beaded on his bald head and ran down into the white fringes around the sides. It made him look as if he was wearing a skull cap. Again Ackors brushed away the dampness and stared at the Labs.

It was 9:04. Damn. The kid should have had time enough by now. What happened if the thing didn't go off and they found it and started backtracking some of the materials? Christ, but that could mean big trouble, and . . .

He saw the flash first, a brilliant strobe light pulse that lit up the morning sky with an added touch of brilliance, cutting through the warm sunshine. From 2 miles away, he watched the smoke and dust billow up long before he heard the sound of the explosion.

Then it came like crackling thunder, diminishing over the miles and rattling away into the country behind him.

Ackors smiled and held the glasses. It had begun, his overt action against the project! Now he had a real chance to disrupt, even destroy the whole program. He'd have to wait and see what his inside man told him about the blast. If the critical stages of the program had been in Building 214 . . . He smiled again just thinking about that. Then he dropped heavily into his Buick and drove back to town.

After parking in his reserved space behind the Mountain State Savings & Loan Association, Ackors went in through the back door and luxuriated in the coolness of the air conditioning. His secretary had been waiting for him. She was 19, not long out of Miss Johnson's secretarial course at Los Alamos High, and as pretty as a springtime daffodil.

These young girl secretaries were fresh, eager, naive and most of them rock dumb. They didn't get in his way and they still could do the job he wanted them to do. The current one's name was Mertha.

"Oh, Mr. Ackors, I have about a dozen calls for you. I put slips on your desk. Two seemed the most important. The Lions president called and said he'd be able to come to your committee meeting tonight on the White Cane fundraiser. Then Mr. Willough said he wanted to combine the next Chamber of Commerce executive meeting with that for the Friends of the Library. All of you are on both boards anyway."

She smiled and followed him into his office as she talked. Now she stood up straighter and deliberately pushed out her breasts.

"Is there anything else, Mr. Ackors?"

"There sure as hell is, but I'd get in trouble with your mother. They're thirty-eights, right?"

She laughed, blushing slightly. "No, Mr. Ackors, I told you thirty-six. And anyway, that's not something . . ." she looked at the open door. "I mean with the door . . ." She turned and walked out quickly.

He sat at his desk and looked at the phone slips. Projects, yes, he had enough public service projects going. Some of them he might be able to let slide if his one big plan had worked this morning.

Mertha stepped back in his office. "Oh, Mr. Ackors, I just heard there's been an explosion out at the Labs, and some of those calls you had were from volunteer firemen. I heard the engine go out about a half an hour ago, and they aren't back yet."

"Thanks, Mertha," he said. She smiled and left after hesitating for just a moment.

When the girl closed the door, he called Dawna Lane.

"Have you heard anything?"

"No," she said in her high, slightly shrill voice. "It's too early yet. It would look suspicious if I called."

"Well, I damn well can't call."

"As a public spirited business leader you could."

"No, we wait until noon. Something should be out

about it by then. Is true love progressing with Dr. Stanley Duyck?"

Her tone was sharp. "Naturally. I know my job and I do it, I'm good at it. You're getting everything I can squeeze out of that scientific weirdo."

"Well squeeze harder. I need to know exactly how far along the development is. I'm getting pressure from upstairs. I needed to know last week. So it's up to you to turn on the charm. Give him a special treatment tonight so he won't even know what he's saying. I need that information tonight."

"I'll try. But he's no junior league cock hound. What's special and wild for someone else is as common as the missionary position to him. I swear, he's insatiable sometimes."

"You two should make a perfect match. Maybe I could get you teamed and we'd make the *Guinness Book of World Records* for constant copulation. Remember, I need everything you can dig out of him by tonight. Call me."

"With a little luck I'll still be able to phone."

She hung up and he put down the phone. Dawna was good at her work, but sometimes he hated her. These Americans became so ridiculously *personal* about all of this. It was just a job.

Dawna had been working with him for almost four years now, and he admitted she had furnished him with 99 percent of his information coming out of the Labs. At first she had been living with the youngest of the eight scientists assigned to Operation LONG REACH. He was a highly perceptive young man and tumbled to her after six weeks. He at last told her to bug off, to leave him, move out. He wasn't going to turn her in for spying or anything, but she asked too many questions, and he wanted her gone.

The next morning the police found Dr. Robert Mahon dead in a tragic auto accident. His car had gone over a cliff and smashed into rubble at the bottom. The girl had been thrown out of the car and clung to a ledge all night.

It was no accident that Dawna knew all eight of the scientists on this project. The men socialized, worked together closely and genuinely liked each other—which made it convenient for Dawna. Even while she was living with Dr. Mahon, Dawna had an affair with another of the big eight, Dr. Bruner. When his wife found out about it, she divorced him at once, took his house and car, and he was so upset about the whole thing, he ran back to his university to teach.

Ackors thought back over the years. He had been there in Los Alamos for ten years, had picked up four different assignments getting information and facts out of the Labs, and was in top standing with his "parent" firm. In town he was known as Mr. Charity, had received the best citizen award twice, the Chamber booster award once, and the Top Lion kudo twice. If only all these sniveling capitalists knew why he had so much time to do their charity work!

Now, it was LONG REACH. He knew exactly what it was all about and had been instructed that the program must be delayed, disrupted, slowed in every possible way without blowing his cover. His ten-year cover was his primary responsibility, but LONG REACH came in as a close second. His own country already had such a weapon as the Americans worked on, but to delay and slow and destroy it if possible would mean the weaponry advantage would last that much longer. He stirred, walked to his window, and back. Basically he was an action man. Sometimes he wished this project had more risks, more danger. His brows went up sharply and he sighed, then went to work on the list of phone calls. He had to maintain his cover as the most public-spirited man in Los Alamos.

When he got home that night from the Labs, Dr. Stanley Duyck sat relaxing in his car a moment. He didn't understand about the attack on the facility that morning, but he did know that it definitely was aimed at LONG REACH. That's what had been bothering him. The FBI had been there, and Dr. Dessel looked as if he was ready to explode, himself. How could anyone outside know about the program? It was top secret. There had never been the hint of any news release about this. Never.

The whole idea of the cold war tensions and the related spying suspicions and dangers were repugnant to Dr. Duyck. He'd been on a vacation to Moscow as a tourist once and had enjoyed it. He liked the warmth of the Russian people. What was all this damned hogwash about spies and secrecy? From the scientific reports and inside material, the men working on this program knew that the Soviets were close to perfecting a similar weapon. So why would there be any static from that quarter?

He got out of the car, took his briefcase, and went up the walk to his house. He'd had an apartment before, but Dawna said they should have a house all to themselves. It would be more like a home for them. So he rented this one at an outlandish price, and it kept the woman happy. He smiled just thinking about Dawna, imagining her fresh from a shower, naked and glowing, wanting him.

He pushed open the front door.

"Hey, anybody home?"

He heard the sliding glass door to the patio close, and she came into the front hall. She'd been suntanning, and baby oil glistened on her brown skin, which was covered slightly by three scraps of cloth they sell for $45 and call a bikini.

She wasn't the prettiest girl he'd ever seen, but she was the sexiest: short brown hair, large almond-shaped green eyes, a small nose, and a cupid mouth in a round face. She stood a slender five-foot-five, with big breasts and a tiny waist over slender, boyish hips. She set one arm on her hip and smiled.

Dr. Duyck dropped his briefcase and laughed low in his throat.

"My God, but you're beautiful and so fucking sexy."

She walked up to him, and he caught the string at her back and pulled it, letting the blue wisps of cloth fall away from her chest.

He bent and kissed each mound. "Now there is one hell of a good set of tits!"

"Yes, I know," she said with a haughty, spoiled, superior, and fake bravado that held up almost through the third word before she giggled and pushed hard against him. He eased her away.

"Wait a minute. First I'm putting you into the shower for an oil change, then I'm prescribing three big injections for you. On second thought, I'll have a shower with you. I hate that damn baby oil."

"Oh, baby, that's what I've been waiting for! I've been lying out there in the sun getting hotter and hotter, and that set me boiling inside. Know what I mean, baby?"

He kissed her breasts again, then pushed her toward the master bathroom.

Two hours later, they lay on the big water bed, too exhausted to move.

"Baby, I wanted to call you this afternoon when I heard about the explosion," Dawna said. "Then I heard on the radio only one person was hurt, a janitor, so I knew you were all right and decided that I shouldn't bother you."

"Yeah, good. The switchboard was jammed for an hour." He rolled over, watching her. How had he lucked out like this? A beautiful, sexy woman with big boobs and a sleek young body and who liked to mess around as much as he did. Only one small problem nagged at him, but he was probably making a big thing out of nothing. So she asked a lot of questions. She was curious.

She turned toward him, her breasts swaying and rolling. "Was it an accident, or do they know? The explosion."

"No accident. A young mentally retarded employee rammed a bomb on his pick-up against the building, and the whole thing exploded. That's about all I know about it."

"Oh! Did it hurt the boy?"

"Hurt him? The explosion and fire ball cremated him instantly. It was so furiously hot, they couldn't even find a bone or a belt buckle left of the kid."

"How horrible!"

"True."

"How's your work coming along?"

"You're not supposed to ask."

"Yeah, I know. But we can't just sit around and

stare at each other. We got to talk. And I know we can't fuck for six hours a day. I thought you might like to talk about it. Other men do."

"Why?"

"I'm no shrink. You said last week you were having some problems. You said dispersion or something like that."

He raised himself up on his elbows and looked at her. "I've never used that word in this house, Dawn. Do you know what it means?"

"What it means? I never heard it before you said it one day. Maybe you was talking in your goddamn sleep, I don't know." She sat up. "Hey! I don't give a damn about your silly old project. I'm just trying to get along, to be good company. To be a real person you can like. Isn't that fair?" He didn't say anything, just reached out and caught one of her breasts.

"If all you want is sex from me, you can stick it up your ass. You can go back down to Flossie's. She's got all kinds and colors of crotches you can fuck off in." Dawna jumped from the bed, scowling now, her fists balled.

"Hey, hey. Easy," he said. "Nobody is carping on you. I had a tough day, and you just wore me down to a nub. Now sit down and relax. Come on, sit down and I'll work on your Ph.D. in physics. Yes, we have the dispersion problem solved. We now have a stream that we can live with at our current target range, so we're moving on to other problems."

She sat at last, her scowl fading. "Yeah, that's great, I guess. So when do we have the celebration party?"

He laughed now and hugged her. "Not for a while

yet. We have a lot more work to do, and the testing."

"But you said the dispersion or whatever was fixed and the range is right. Hey, what's a range? Like with cattle on it, or like in the kitchen?"

He shook his head in amazement. "No, like in distance, a thousand yards, a mile, five hundred miles."

"Wow, you've got a five-hundred-mile range?"

He rolled out of the bed and stood over her where she sat on the edge.

"Now that is one goddamned time too many! I made a list this afternoon. You are just too good to be true. First, you were sleeping with Bob Mahon when he gets himself killed in his car wreck, while you get away without a scratch. Then you broke up Dr. Bruner's marriage, and he ran home to Cal Tech. Now you're doing the live-in bit with me. What are you, the project whore?" He looked at her, but she didn't even flinch.

"All three of us working at the Labs, and all three on the same fucking project. How do you account for that?" He paused as she looked up. "No, don't tell me yet. I've been doing some remembering. This isn't the first time that you've come up with some questions about things I've never mentioned. Dispersion, range, maximum velocity, working voltage, silver windings. Then one night you convinced me you knew nothing about how a betatron worked. It's just too damn much."

"I didn't use those words, I don't even . . ."

"Shut up, Dawna. After that innocent slow-witted kid killed himself out there today, I did some more serious thinking. Something is just as rotten as hell in this whole arrangement. I should have caught on about three months ago, but I'm slow. When your tits are big and your cunt tight, I am naturally slow to want to change the old routine."

She rolled across the bed away from him and stood, still naked. "Baby, I don't know what you're talking about. You're the best lay around here."

"Bullshit, Dawna. You took me for a ride."

"I don't understand."

"Understand? Hell, you understand all right. You've been pumping me for classified information, on a top secret project. All I need to do is find out who your contact is, who you report to, and I'll pull the plug on this whole damned spy apparatus."

She bent, opened the night stand, pulled out a small automatic, and snicked off the safety.

"Oh, yes, baby. It's loaded and I know how to use it." Her expression was hard now, all acting, all pretense gone.

He sighed and sat down on the bed. "I'll be a son-of-a-bitch. It's true. I was fishing, I was bluffing you, and I know that you're a piss-poor poker player. I bluff and you raise the goddamn ante with an automatic. I wasn't sure about you, but too many things started to fit together." He glared at her, then his expression changed to pity. He stood, walked around the bed, and held out his hand. "I'll take the gun, Dawna. You don't have the guts to pull the trigger, let alone shoot someone."

She lifted the automatic expertly and fired once as he moved toward her. The round took him over the right eye, drove into his brain, shattered and ripped through hundreds of vital nerve endings, patterns, and centers. He fell on the bed bleeding and died in 20 seconds.

Ten minutes after Dr. Stanley Duyck died, Harry Ackors walked casually through the vacant lot behind Duyck's rented house and slipped in the back door. He listened intently as Dawna explained it, nodded and then frowned.

"Three times is too many," he said. "But we'll have to live with it. You're off this case. And within a week, I want you out of town. But only after you're cleared of any involvement by the police. Get me a bucket of water."

She did. They didn't move Dr. Duyck from where he had fallen and bled on the water bed. All Ackors did was examine the back of Duyck's head to be sure the bullet had not gone all the way through.

He held the muzzle of the automatic against the pillow, so the bullet would go through it, muffled the sound with the rest of the pillow, and fired into the bucket of water. Then he dropped the pillow on the floor beside the bed.

They emptied the bucket of water, and Ackors took the spent slug and put it in his pocket.

"Now, Dawna, give me five minutes to get out the back door, then I want you to get into your robe and call the police. Don't get dressed, not yet. And, Dawna, try to work up a little believable hysteria this time, can you? Otherwise you might get yourself hung for murder."

Chapter 3

WASH AND FLUFF DRY FREE

Mark Hardin worked steadily in the overheated desert sun, wearing only cutoff jeans and heavy shoes. Sweat glistened on his skin as he laid up blocks on the long wall that slowly took shape and now was 3 feet high on the cement slab. Mark put down his trowel and snapped the taut level line, then placed the 6 foot aluminum straightedge against the center of a row of blocks. He smiled.

"Hey, Randy. Looking damn fine, man! You'll be ready to turn pro as soon as we get this building up."

The young Indian working to his right was almost as tall as Mark Hardin's six-two-and-a-half, but he was thinner and wiry.

"Hell, by then it'll be time for me to take a month's break, Raincloud." The kid was in his late teens, maybe 20, and of all the men who had agreed to help on this community bath house and laundry building, Randy had been the best. He had learned to lay up the 8 by 8 by 16-inch cement blocks quickly and professionally. He could get a job with a masonry contractor if he tried.

Mark stood back and admired the project. It was a building 24 feet wide and 32 feet long. At each end would be showers, lavatories, and wash basins. In the 12-foot center section would go a row of automatic washers and dryers, bought with tribal funds and managed by the elders.

The Morongo Indian reservation 20 miles from Palm Springs was far from the richest reservation in the state. Mark went there every chance he had, and lately he had been working on this project. He had talked with the tribal elders and got permission to put up the building. Then it was a matter of the design, getting in the plumbing, and then pouring the slab.

Mark had paid for everything, and now the men of the tribe were pitching in to put up the blocks. They were building it solidly, with reinforcing steel and poured sections to fill up the hollow blocks. The community bath house should stand for 200 years.

Six men worked on the wall, some mixing mud, some putting the mortar up for the block layers, and three setting the blocks with Mark. It was going better than he expected. Three more good days, and they should be ready to put up the beams.

An insistent tone came from his back pocket. Mark took the pack-of-cigarettes-sized radio from his jeans and pressed a red button. The tone stopped, and a moment later a woman's voice came over the speaker.

"J-34, contact your office at once. That's J-34 to a land line and contact your office."

The radio went silent. Mark put it back in his pocket as one of the men looked up and laughed.

"Looks like you bought yourself some more trouble, Raincloud. I bet every time that beeper goes off you get troubles."

"You noticed," Mark said. He put down the trowel and waved at the men. "Keep it moving. I'll be right back."

Mark was a larger, more powerful man than he seemed to be at first glance. He was heavily muscled and looked like an athlete in training. His general complexion was dark and now suntanned to a coppery brown. He could move with the supple litheness of a cougar, and his dark eyes gave his face, even in repose, a smoldering, critical look. When he frowned, a lethal aura seemed to surround him.

Hardin's usual hair coloring was a deep black, but for security reasons, he now had his hair and eyebrows bleached out to near blond. He had shaved off his moustache. Mark still wore his hair long, covering his ears, and his weight was a steady 209 pounds. His accent, if any, was NBC news commentator, but Easterners usually detected a bit of far-west twang if they listened closely.

Mark walked a half-block through the desert dust to the Shell station, where the pumps showed the tourist price at $1.12 a gallon for unleaded. The tribe-run station pumped the same gas to Indians for 83 cents a gallon.

Mark waved at the attendant and stepped into the phone booth just off U.S. Highway 10 and dialed. A few moments later, he talked to Professor Willard Haskins in the Stronghold.

"Professor. Mark."

"Good, good. I'm glad it worked."

"Since when did I become J-34?"

"I thought it was a good idea, vaguely indicating Justice Department. And it was only an experiment, but it did work out quite well. Now I know I can contact you with the beeper over at least half of the United States. We're using a stationary satellite repeater, a commercial satellite, so we simply pay for the call. It's just like the repeaters the local police and business radio use, except our repeater is parked up there a hundred and eighty-five miles in synchronous earth orbit."

"The wonders of modern science," Mark said with a grin in his voice. "But it does work. Is this just a test?"

"Not at all, my boy. You've been gone four days, and some things need looking at. You also had a phone call from someone called J. Tabler. Then two other matters have reached the critical state on our project board, and I think you should review them in person. You may want to take on one or the other as a new case."

"The same two we've been watching?"

"One of the same, and a new one. It seems there was a large explosion in the Los Alamos Scientific Laboratories, where they do a lot of national defense research work. It was labeled pure and simple sabotage, but no one seems to have any idea who made the attack or why."

"Sounds interesting. I'll get my crew set for the next few days and drive back there tonight. What did Tabler say?"

"Just that she wants you to call her. She also happens to be in New Mexico, in Los Alamos, to be exact."

Mark laughed. "Figures. It's hard to stay ahead of Justice Department people, isn't it?"

They said good-bye and hung up. Mark spent the next half-hour explaining to Randy exactly how he wanted the blocks laid up. Randy had a schematic showing the windows and doors and had the frames to build in as they moved along.

After washing up at an open faucet, Mark put on

a clean pair of pants and a T-shirt, then gunned his no-make 1977 pick-up down the dusty trail to the highway. The desert rig was mostly Ford 300 pick-up, but also a little bit of Chevy, Dodge, and Jeep that Mark had put together to make a four-wheel power wagon that could go almost anywhere in the desert and pack a camper as well.

Right now the bare Brown Beast was painted a rust brown, with an under-hood 427 Ford V-8 gas guzzler, a finely tuned engine aimed at both power and performance.

He wondered what Joanna was doing in New Mexico. Was she on the sabotage case at the highly secret and sensitive Los Alamos Scientific Labs? He knew a lot of atomic research had gone on there, as well as other highly classified work. He smiled thinking about Tabler. She was a friend of long standing. He'd first met her when she held a gun to his head in a car and demanded information. She was a Justice Department field agent and a good one.

He gunned the Brown Beast down the ramp to U.S. 10 and moved out at a steady 55 miles per hour for Beaumont, Redlands, and then San Bernardino. There he would take U.S. 15 north for Barstow and the Stronghold. He had a little over a hundred miles to go. Mark flipped on the Los Angeles all-news radio station, KNX, and settled down to driving. He should roar into the Stronghold just before dark.

In the Stronghold, Professor Haskins watched the visual blips on his area display board show the progression of a vehicle through the audio checkpoint fence along the access road to the black-topped air strip. He caught a video fix on the rig as it rounded the corner toward the airstrip in the fading light, and identified it as the Brown Beast. It was probably Mark. They had this elaborate security system, so it only made sense to use it.

A half-hour later, Mark had showered and shaved, and he sat at a dinner of blood-rare venison steak and vegetables. He ate slowly as he looked over the sheaf of reports in a file folder beside his plate. Both David Red Eagle and the Professor left him alone as he ate and studied the reports.

The first folder was about loan sharkings, the harassment, and the other related terror tactics, right up to mayhem and murder, in the Mexican-American barrio in the Dallas–Fort Worth area. The problem had reached such massive proportions, the local police were asking for state help. Six killings had taken place in a two-week period, and all were poor Mexicans who had borrowed money they had no way to pay back.

Mark finished the venison, then looked at the second folder. It held the police wire teletype report on the bombing at Los Alamos. He read it carefully. One death was reported, but there were no suspects and no evidence left; the bomb totally vaporized all triggering devices and the pick-up driver. The only lead was the identity of the driver, that he was a borderline mentally retarded youth of 19 and easily led. The boy was undoubtedly used by someone and had no idea what the importance was of his actions.

Mark was interested in the concluding paragraph.

"The attack took place in a restricted area on a secret project. Not even the name of the project has been released or can now be made known. Labs director Dr. William Dessel says to know that this building was being used for the secret work would have meant inside information was obtained. He stressed that this was a matter of great concern, and was involving a national defense matter of grave importance."

Mark tapped the folder and went on reading. He had a story from a newspaper that reported that the Soviets were deep into research that could lead to a killer ray, a death beam kind of weapon straight out of Flash Gordon. Another news story denied that the United States was working on any such "monstrous" weapon, but speculated that it was the type of weaponry that the Soviet Union would develop.

A third news clipping gave more details, showing that a laser weapon was a short-range, high-energy type of device. If and when it was developed, it would be a weapon for use up to 100 or perhaps 200 yards at the most. This scientist said the only logical type of long-range "death ray" would be a charged particle beam that would fire atomic particles such as protons or neutrons at the speed of light down an aimed narrow beam that would destroy the target. It didn't say what these atomic particles would do in the target, and Mark had no idea how it might work.

The article continued, saying that "Jane's Weapons Systems" report, the international monitor and publisher of the latest up-to-the-minute evaluation of weapons on all world powers, said there was no evidence that any nation had a completed, functioning "ray gun" at this time, but it was believed that two or more major powers were researching such weapons.

The article concluded by saying that, in this scientist's opinion, an accelerated charged particle beam would be a practical and obtainable strategic weapon for either of the big powers, and if the United States were working on such a program, it would undoubtedly be through the Los Alamos Scientific Laboratories in New Mexico, where much of the research on U.S. atomic bombs and other advanced weapons had been done.

Mark put down the reports. Now he saw why the Professor had grouped the "death ray" file with that of the sabotage at the Los Alamos Labs. Speculation, but with a positive kind of feel. It might be worth a look to see what he could find out. If the Russians did have a team of agents there trying to knock down development on such a particle beam weapon, it sounded like a project where he could do some good.

And there was Tabler. Why was she really there? To watch this project? He pushed his chair away from the table, took all the folders, and went up to his desk in the tower room. There he picked up a phone, and a few moments later his direct dialing had the connection made with Joanna.

"Me. Tabler?"

"Yes, Mark?"

"True. And you're right, it's been far, far too long. What are you doing out here in the wild west, away from the culture and sophistication of the big city?"

"I'm on a vacation. At least that's what Dan Griggs calls it. I'm keeping tabs on a group called the Western Naturalists United. I've trailed them from Seattle to Provo, and now down here, or is it up or over here? This is a kind of Super Sierra Club of do-gooders, only these goons have guts and sharp claws. They knock heads, burn down buildings, kidnap people, threaten and intimidate anybody to promote their selected environmental ideas. I've been monitoring them for almost a year now, and we can't get anything on them that will hold up in court. So we decided on an infiltration. They said they were coming down here to close up Los Alamos Labs, that they are inherently antinature, therefore evil."

"Sound like real sweethearts. Is that all you're there for?"

"As far as I know. Unless Dan is being super sneaky."

"What about that sabotage there today?"

"It couldn't have been my bunch. They just began straggling into town this afternoon. Most of them hitchhike. One bitchy broad who runs the outfit drives a Continental. No, I don't see how they could have been involved unless some came in early."

"Possible."

"Are you interested in that explosion?"

"I'm an explosion freak, you know that, Tab. Besides, the blast incinerated a retarded young man and blew up a top secret program building. Damn right I'm interested."

"So why don't you fly over tonight? We can have a small reunion, and you can check things."

He'd been thinking the same thing. "Why don't you call Dan and get him to wire you a set of Department of Justice I.D. confirmations for me as Keith Zilke. I already have the name and the cards used before. Get me Top Secret and Need-to-Know clearances, for the accelerated-beam weapon program. Send that last one directly to Dr. William Dessel, the head man at the Labs."

"You don't ask for much, do you?"

"Only when I can get it." He paused and pictured

her platinum blonde hair, short and frilly, and her large hazel eyes.

"Okay, I'll try with Dan. He might not like it, but I should be able to talk him into it. You might be persuaded to give me a hand with my environmental freakies. Besides, he owes you one, right?"

"One? He owes me about a dozen favors."

"I'll remind him. I'm staying at the Plaza Motel, but I'm trying to infiltrate that bunch of jokers, so I'll probably be living with them at some rented house. They usually find one, and everybody crashes. That's their usual M.O., so if I'm not here when you come, leave a message, from . . . Brownie."

"Right, Blondie. I'll see you in the morning, or as soon as I can get there."

Chapter 4

HEAD-BUSTING DO-GOODERS

Joanna Tabler parked a block from the address she had taken over the phone and evaluated the poorly painted, rubble-strewn yards in this rundown section of Los Alamos. It wasn't Park Avenue. A long-haired dog, German shepherd size but of varied heritage and with big splotches of hair falling out, started to attack her from behind a gate swinging on one hinge, but the dog lost interest and turned back into the yard, whining when Joanna showed no fear.

Joanna had left her .38 and mace in her suitcase. No use taking any chances on the first real contact. But she had brought something more important to her acceptance by the wild-eyed conservationist group—an envelope with five new $100 bills inside.

She spotted the right house before she could read the number. Sitting well back from the street, the two-story affair was about 50 years old, wooden with lots of gingerbread, and probably was the talk of the town when it was built. Now it needed paint and lawn work, everything but one more resident.

A just-polished, new Lincoln Continental parked at the curb looked curiously out of place. It had California plates and an Auto Club sticker. Tabler walked up the cracked sidewalk and looked for a doorbell, but found only a twist knob of black metal and turned it, producing a mechanical ringing sound.

When the door opened, a long-haired youth stood looking at her. He wore only boxer undershorts with large red hearts on them.

"Yeah?" his voice was scratchy, neutral.

"I'm Melissa. Rivers said she wanted to see me."

"You're too damn old."

"You're too damn young. Tell Rivers I'm here, or take me to her. Don't you have any sense, or are you just plain weird?"

The kid grinned. Joanna figured he was about 17. His hand came from his back, and she saw the roach stuck with a long pin. Then she smelled the sweetness of the smoke. He waved her inside, the grin not changing. When the door closed, he took a long drag on the roach and pointed toward a closed door across the big living room. The stringy-haired youth still held the pot smoke in his lungs as she walked to the door.

Joanna knocked.

"It's open, for Christ's sakes, think this is a goddamned bank or something?" The voice came through the panel plainly. Somebody behind her snickered. Tabler opened the door and stepped inside. She knew at once she was overdressed in her sleek white pants suit, white shoes, and frilly light yellow blouse and scarf. H. R. Rivers wore a man's white shirt with nothing under it and the tails flapping over tight, much washed and patched blue jeans. She was barefoot and smoking a tailormade.

What caught Tabler's interest was the woman's eyes. They were small, tightly set in her face, so dark that they seemed black, and she had no eyebrows at all, just thin lines of mascara. Her mouth was small, and the lips now pressed into a frown. Rivers was a tiny woman, no more than five-foot-one, slender, flat chested, and with a head of long, straight, black hair.

"Sorry, I've got a shitty mouth. You're Melissa, right?" She held out her hand. It was hard and thin like the rest of her.

"Yes, and you're H. R. Rivers. I want to join the Western Naturalists United. I talked to you in Provo, and you said if I was going to be over this way . . ."

"Yeah, right." She rubbed her face and walked to the window, then looked back at Tabler. "You just don't look like one of us. Too pretty, too rich looking. Why are you here?"

"Because you get things done! You don't just fuck around talking. You're an action group, and that's the only thing that's going to save this country from the conglomerates, from the industrial-governmental-econoblock. You people care about our land and our water and our air."

"Yeah, Melis, not bad." She frowned, then raised her brows. "Well, I guess we can dirty you up a little."

Now Tabler noticed that the room had no furniture except one chair. A sleeping bag in the corner had not been unrolled.

Rivers squatted on the floor, then sat down, her back hard against the wall, legs spraddled. "Now, Melis, why the hell are you really here?"

Tabler slumped to the floor, her off-white pants getting dirty, but that was part of the show.

"Hell, Rivers, you know. I told you on the phone. My old man owns a cement plant, and the dust that comes out of it is ruining a whole section of farmland. I tried to get him to put on some dust collectors. I got the state clean air board after him, and then some of my friends and I picketed the plant. He had us all thrown in jail..."

"Yeah, but then he bailed you out. Did you bring anything for me?"

Tabler took the envelope from her small purse, tore off the end, and spread out five new $100 bills on the floor.

"I said a thousand, Melis."

"Five hundred was all I could get."

"Sell your car."

"I rode over here on the bus. I don't have a car. Right now I'm driving a rented Pinto."

Rivers sighed. "Dammit, I told you a thousand initiation fee." Rivers pouted for a moment. "Shit. Five hundred is enough this time. Just so you fit in and do as you're told." The woman's eyes softened then, as she looked at Joanna. Her eyes tarried too long on Joanna's breasts, then swept down to her hips and paused again. For just a moment, Tabler wondered if the young woman were gay.

Both women stood.

"Well, Melis, you're a member of Western Naturalists United. Find a spot to crash out there. Everyone stays in this shack. We've got ten rooms and one bath that doesn't work, so we'll rough it. We don't bother having the electricity turned on. The people like candles better. You got a sleeping bag?"

Tabler shook her head.

"I keep a couple of extras in my trunk. I'll have one sent up for you. Can you cook?"

"A little."

"Good, I'm poison city when it comes to cooking. We could use some more food if you've got any cash left." Rivers watched her for a minute. "Honey, get the fuck out of those fancy clothes, quick. Jeans and a tight T-shirt goes best around here."

"Then I can stay? I can work with you?"

"For this gig. When it's done, we'll need another five hundred bucks for the next stop."

"Yes, fine. I'll be able to get more then. I'll go get my bag at the car and be right back."

"Right. Get the clothes changed first thing."

Tabler was well aware that H. R. Rivers watched closely as she walked out of the room.

A tall black kid about 23 sat near the door in the hall, watching for her.

"Clutch," he said standing up. She thought he'd never stop unbending. Clutch was over six-foot-six. The name and size stirred a memory.

She shook his hand, and when she did he pulled her in quickly and kissed her lips. "Oh, yeah, Mamma! But you are one fine looking bundle of woman. I hear you're staying."

Tabler stepped back and grinned, trying not to let the sudden kiss upset her. "Yes, isn't it great? Rivers says I'm in!"

"Oh, Mamma, that's where I'd like to be!" Clutch said. He laughed. "Hey, got to go get some stuff? Clutch can help."

"Sure."

They went out the door.

"How long you been with Ms. Rivers?"

"Six months, maybe seven. She's got good grass, and it's no hassle, so why not?"

"And she really is doing a lot of good for the environment."

"Oh, hell yes, that too."

His brows lifted at the rented Pinto. She told him she had to take it back the next day, since her daddy paid the rent. They both laughed and went back to the old house, Clutch carrying her flight bag.

"Upstairs front is your room," he told her. "I kind of lay on the room assignments."

Now Tabler saw others of the group. There were more girls than men. Most of them looked to be in their late teens, and a few in their early twenties. There were a dozen kids in the living room, with jeans and T-shirts the uniform of the day. Most of the girls had long, stringy, unwashed hair. Half the men had long hair, and nearly all had beards. Some of them looked up and nodded. Others were obviously strung out on pot or something else. She wondered if Rivers furnished all the goods.

Up the stairs they saw more people, then Clutch turned into a room. "Here's our place," Clutch said. He pushed open a door to the bedroom. It had no furniture, but it did boast an old carpet on the floor and two windows. Already four sleeping bags were in the room. He tossed her plastic airline carryall on a dirty blue sleeping bag.

"You want another sack, or is one enough?"

"Rivers said something about having one for me in her car."

"Right, I'll go get it. Make yourself at home."

He left and Tabler dug out the Greenpeace T-shirt and quickly took off her pants top and blouse, then stripped off her bra as well and pulled on the T-shirt. That should be more in style.

A boy and a girl came in, ignored her, and fell on one of the sleeping bags, locked in a furious and heated kiss. The boy rolled on top of the girl, and Tabler saw his hand rubbing her breasts. She looked away.

Clutch came in just then and grinned.

"Don't pay them no shit, they don't even know we're here." He looked at her. "Oh, Mamma, I like that T-shirt. You've got great boobs. Now, where are the jeans?"

She held them up.

"Well, change into them. We've got a briefing in ten minutes."

"Where do I change?"

"Here, dammit. This is your space."

She waited a minute, but he didn't leave. She smiled, turned around, and stripped off her white pants. As she folded them, she felt his hand run along her bottom.

"Oh, nice!" he said. Now, come on, it's almost time for the briefing."

She slid into the jeans, buttoned them, and went to the door. Clutch prodded the pair on the sleeping bag.

"Break it up, you nookie-hounds. Miz Rivers is about to lay down the word."

The pair on the floor untangled and stood up with no comment or reaction. A Rivers call evidently was a command.

Downstairs, about 20 young people sat around the living room floor. A small fire had been built in the old fireplace, and H. R. Rivers sat in front of it, wearing the same clothes she had before. When the group settled down and quieted, she turned and began like an old-time preacher, only with a different vocabulary.

"We are not here to fuck around!"

"Right!" the group answered.

"We are here to close down the Los Alamos Scientific Laboratories, where they are doing outlandish things to our God-given air and the environment."

"Hey, right on, H. R.!" someone said.

"I mean, this is a ridiculous complex of brilliant young scientists out there polluting our atmosphere, making atomic things we don't even understand, and maybe even working on biological weapons, for all we know. We won't permit it to continue!"

"Hey, hey, right on!" the chorus answered.

"This pseudo scientific, big-business-dominated government is ruining everything it touches. Our air isn't safe, our beaches aren't safe, and God knows that nothing we're offered to eat in the supermarkets or restaurants is anywhere near safe or healthy for our bodies. We've got to charge into this military-industrial-government complex and fight them with everything we have.

"Big business, big science, and big government are reducing the citizen to that of a fifteenth or twentieth rate citizen. We're pawns in their hands, led to the slaughter for the glory of their princes and horsemen and bishops and queens.

"We've got to struggle and break out of this status quo of being totally dominated by a government that is antienvironment, by politicians who don't give a shit about anything but getting reelected every term, and bureaucrats who love to do nothing if they can get by with it, or write reports that have no value and significance about someone else writing reports on equally inconsequential affairs."

She looked around. "We aren't here just for the kicks. We're not here for the free pot and a little messing around on the side. We are here to put our minds and bodies on the line, to show these business bastards that they can't shove the people around anymore. Power to the people!"

The group took up the cry, repeating it a dozen times. Then she smiled, held up her hands, and nodded.

"Yes, power to the people, and we are the people, and we do have the power. All we have to do is to use it, to show them. We might have to knock a few heads until they realize it, but they will if we work. We can show them that whales are important, that the whooping crane is valuable, that clean air is a heritage, that atomic power is a catastrophe, that porpoise are not trash fish, and that one simple atomic reactor accident can spew future death into the atmosphere and blight unborn babies and damage the genetic ability of all children for a dozen generations! Take the Three Mile Island plant at Harrisburg as an example. Remember it? The cooling system breakdown, a valve malfunctioned and the first thing we know, radiation is being detected in the air twenty miles away. Twenty goddamned fucking miles! And within one mile of that plant there are fifteen thousand residents! What's happening to those people?

"You remember how it came about. Radioactive water was released to an auxiliary building, where "clean" water is normally cooled. Then plant officials vented steam from the building without even knowing it was radioactive. These sons-of-bitches weren't even smart enough to know how their own plant operated or what they were doing!

"Now, according to our reports there is something going on out at these Labs here that would make the Three Mile Island disaster look like a Sunday afternoon box social. They're dealing with something out there that would annihilate whole cities, something that could be fired at the earth from *space*! And we're going to stop it. We don't have to know exactly what it is, but that explosion we heard about yesterday had something to do with it. So get ready. You're soldiers, and we might have some casualties on our side, but it's important. We need a victory here to put these scientist freaks on notice that the people have the power, and now we're going to use it!"

"Power to the people! Power to the people! Power to the people!" The chant continued as the meeting broke up.

Clutch had been sitting beside Tabler on the floor. He helped her up and then led her to the stairs.

"Hey, Mamma, you really dig all that power to the people jazz?"

"Why do you think I'm here, Clutch?"

"Damned if I know, Mamma. You're so old."

She slapped him gently. "Never tell a girl that, Clutch, just never."

"You over thirty?"

"You over fifteen, you black son-of-a-bitch?" she asked, smiling.

He roared with laughter and pulled her up the stairs. They went into the room they had left earlier. The couple who had been on the sleeping bag before were there again, already both were bare to the waist.

"Hey, Mamma, time we get to know each other better. I bet you give good head."

He slid his hand over one of her breasts, his thumb twanging her nipple back and forth.

Tabler reacted almost without thinking. She

caught his far arm, pulled him toward her, bending his wrist back toward his palm, threw out her hip, and flipped him neatly on the sleeping bag. He hit hard, yelped, and rolled to his hands and knees. His anger faded and he laughed.

"Look, Clutch. I don't mess around with fifteen-year-old basketball stars," she said. "You played with the Nets two years as Clutch Washington. You had a good inside move to the basket, but you fouled out in more games than any other player in the NBA. You scored well but fucked up on defense, and that's what got your ass busted back to the bench."

She had her hands on her hips staring down at him. "Now cool it, hot and ready. I got to do some food shopping for Rivers to stock up the larder. You stay cool and I might come back. What I'm saying, big man, is don't rush the hell out of me. I've never done this salt and pepper jazz, so don't rush me, or you'll foul out of this game, too."

He sat back, laughing softly. "Shit, you do remember. Not many of our fans even did. You must have been in New York."

"Back then. Now shoot up or something. I'll be back."

She went out of the room and down the steps to the front door without talking to anyone. There didn't seem to be any tail on her or a watch on her car. She raced back the other way in the Pinto and called her motel at a filling station. Yes, there was a message. Brownie was looking for her.

Joanna felt a surge of excitement as she drilled the Pinto through the small town to the Plaza Motel and slanted into a parking slot. She tried her motel room door, expecting it to be unlocked. It wasn't.

Her key got her inside, and there he was, lying on the bed, reading a sheaf of papers.

Joanna gawked in amazement.

"You're blond?" she yelped.

"I'm trying to see if they really do have more fun."

A moment later she was in his arms, kissing his long-remembered lips and holding him so tight, she never wanted to let go of him again.

Chapter 5

HELLO, MR. GOODMAN!

Joanna and Mark laughed and kissed again, then she leaned back from him.

"I don't have much time, Mark. First, I think I like you as a blond. I'll let you know for sure later. Now business. I called Dan Griggs, and he bitched and groaned but finally said he'd send you clearance, even though this is the FBI's baby. You're here simply as an observer and not supposed to make any waves. Use the I.D. you have as Keith Zilke. He even wrangled a Top Security clearance and a Need-to-Know on the project with the Labs director."

Mark kissed her cheek and held her tightly.

"I'm just getting involved with this action-environment group. I had my first interview and greased a palm with some cash, so I'm on the inside for this caper. That means I have to crash in their rented house on Ivy Street, and I get to use their sleeping bags. I also have to buy some food before I go back. Snack foods should work best, since there's no heat or electricity in the place. Maybe hot soup over a candle?"

Mark watched her as she talked, the same soft platinum blonde hair, short and stylish, framing her beautiful face. Hazel eyes dominated her face, revealing her moods and feelings all too plainly sometimes, and now brimming with love and tenderness.

"I'll use your pad tonight and see what I can stir up tomorrow. If this is a wild goose chase, I'll see if I can help you get something that will stick on the Rivers woman."

The next morning, Mark checked the town's paper, the *News-Leader,* at the newspaper office. By 8:18 he had read all about the explosion the day before. There wasn't much. He talked with the only reporter in the news room and found out some other interesting facts about the Labs in the news. The reporter was about 30, blond, with glasses and a short haircut. Hans Running was his name.

"Hey, did you hear about the suicide? One of the scientists who worked out at the Labs shot himself. A pretty big wheel out there, from what I heard. The FBI is on it and everything. It will be out in the afternoon issue."

"A real suicide?"

"That's what our sheriff says it looks like. I just saw the galley proof on it. You want to read it?"

Mark said he would, took the long proof, and read it through. "It doesn't say what project he was working on, just that his work is classified. You find out the project?"

"Nope. Everything out there is classified, including the garbage detail. They give me a pain sometimes. But it's federal, and you know how the government screws up everything. You know about the other guy from the Labs who died, too, don't you? That was six, maybe eight months ago. This guy was a Ph.D. too—of course most of them are out there, I guess. This one got himself creamed in a car wreck. Hey, that triggers a thought. Let me check the old file copy."

Running went to the newspapers that hung on a wooden rack and were kept in sequence by long wooden sticks that clamped together on the end. He searched through the last one, didn't find what he needed, and took a look in a huge bound volume that held the full-sized newspapers. He leafed through a while, then grinned.

"Take a look at this page, sport."

The story was on the front page, with a picture of a car that had rolled and smashed and been battered almost to pieces. The roof couldn't be identified, two wheels had broken off, and all the windows were smashed out. A picture of a pretty girl next to the wreck shot caught his attention.

The caption read: "Dawna Lane after she told police her harrowing tale of rolling down Butte Canyon Road in the car at left. She suffered only a bloody nose and a few scratches. Police said it was a miracle she survived. Her companion in the vehicle, Dr. Robert Mahon, was killed in the crash. Police are still investigating."

Mark looked up. "What does this have to do with the suicide?"

Running scowled. "I'm not sure, but I am positive as hell that I'm going to find out. That same girl, Dawna Lane, was the one who found Dr. Stanley Duyck's body and reported it. Isn't that a curious coincidence?"

"Damn curious. Do you have any idea what projects these two men were working on?"

"I've heard rumors. An AP wire deskman from Denver phoned me the other day wanting a thousand words on something called Operation LONG REACH at the Labs. I tried to call, but they were surprised that I even knew the name and said they couldn't talk to me about it. They said I shouldn't know about the project, and they would appreciate a simple 'no comment' to the AP deskman."

"That's the name of something out there—I've heard it before." Mark paused. "You know anything more about this Dawna Lane? Any dirt, any gossip?"

"No, except she's a good-looking, sexy broad," Running said.

Mark bought a copy of the paper and went outside. He drove around the small town until he found the sheriff's office and parked. He shivered slightly as he walked through the doors. Going inside any police facility did that to him now. If only they knew who he was, he'd be in jail in 20 seconds.

A bright young deputy waved. "Help you?"

Mark brought out his Department of Justice buzzer and waved it at the deputy. "Yes, matter of fact you can. Zilke, U.S. Justice Department. We're interested in this suicide you had last night. Who is the investigator on that case? I'd like to talk with him for a while."

"Oh, that one. The sheriff did that one himself. I don't think he's busy if you'd like to see him."

Sheriff Bill Logan was not pleased. His jowls were heavy and sagging, throwing his face out of balance. He was tall and fat—at six-foot-four and 290 pounds he could look down on most men. He stubbed out a cigarette and lit another one. The ash tray overflowed.

"Department of Justice?" he asked looking at the badge. "Just what the bloody hell is going on here? First that explosion, now a suicide and the FBI and the Justice Department. What happened to the CIA, are they late?"

"This is just routine for us, sir. The FBI has the basic jurisdiction. We're just back-up for them. Whenever one of our vital defense and experimental sites is hit like this, it gets everyone in Washington all scattered to the winds. You know the scam, sir."

"Hell, I guess I do. What can I help you with?"

"The death. Are you sure it was a suicide?"

"Looks good right now. No powder burns on the victim, but there was a pillow with powder burns all over it. The witness said he held it to his head and fired right through the pillow. No reason we should disbelieve our one eye witness."

"Unless she shot him, of course. What do you know about the girl?"

The sheriff sighed and looked up, shrugged and passed a file to Mark. "She's not local, came here couple of years ago. We don't know a hell of a lot more. Works part time at some savings and loan. Had been living with this scientist guy but not married. We ran a check on her prints but got back no matches from the state file or from the FBI."

"No local record?"

"Nope, she's clean as a whistle."

"What about an auto wreck six to eight months ago? Her companion was killed. They rolled down Butte Canyon Road."

Sheriff Logan looked up quickly. "By God! You're right. One of my men thought at the time something looked a little out of sync there, but he couldn't make anything out of it, so it went down as accidental. She was the same girl, wasn't she? And she was living with him without benefit of clergy, as we used to say."

Mark looked through the reports. "She says the deceased came home depressed because of some problem at work. He didn't want to talk about it. That night he got ready for bed early, then changed his mind, put the pillow to his head and shot himself through the pillow. Then she said she ran to the phone and called the sheriff."

"She hasn't changed her story in any way in ten hours. And of course it's her word, and we don't have any evidence, or any other witnesses...."

"Yes, I know. Sheriff, would you do me a favor? Would you run her prints in some other states? New York, Illinois, California, Nevada, Florida, and maybe Arizona. I could get the department to do it, but I think I've seen her somewhere before."

"Right, Zilke. That won't cost me anything. And while we're at it, we'll see what else we can dig up on her locally."

"Thanks, Sheriff. I'll stay in touch."

Mark let out one short sigh of relief when he walked out the door of the sheriff's office into the morning sunshine. Those law and order places still made him nervous.

He drove the rented Fairmont past the scene of the suicide, but found a sheriff's car still outside. He was in no rush to meet this girl, not yet. In a small town like this, it wasn't unnatural for most of the people to know most of the other folks. And if she had been sleeping with one of the Lab scientists, it was reasonable that they would have socialized, and in that way she could have gotten to know Stanley Duyck. After her first lover cashed in, she could have looked around and picked out Duyck as the next best candidate for a meal ticket. Possible.

Mark drove to the Labs. He'd never been there before and was surprised at the pleasant atmosphere, the almost parklike feeling at the place. Five minutes after he arrived, he was shown into the director's office, checked out on his clearances including his Need-to-Know order signed by the Attorney General himself.

Dr. Dessel grimaced. He wasn't used to being investigated and certainly didn't like to get orders and static from anyone other than those in his own chain of command. But a damned DOJ order was legal, and he had to obey it.

Reluctantly, he sketched in the bare minimum of details on Project LONG REACH.

"This LONG REACH work, Mr. Zilke, is highly specialized. It is a top secret, long-range, charged atomic particle beam. It fires protons, neutrons, or electrons out of a betatron, which have been accelerated to tremendous speeds that are usually about ninety-six percent of the speed of light. The beam is not a "death ray," but it can have devastating effects on the target. We're looking at it primarily as a defensive weapon for the United States. For example, with a series of these LONG REACH weapons on satellites in synchronous orbits over us, we could totally destroy an ICBM attack or individually targeted MERV clusters. This weapon has the potential of neutralizing an enemy's missile offensive nuclear force with a fantastically high percentage of accuracy. Of course, planes would be sitting ducks for this weapon."

"Dr. Dessel, do our potential enemies also have such a weapon?"

"We're not sure. We know they're working on one. Jane's Directory says no nation now has such a weapons system, but the editors can't be one hundred percent sure, and it could have been developed since the last report."

"Then it is conceivable that some other power might try to stop or sabotage your work here?"

"It is possible and probable."

"Were Dr. Duyck and a Dr. Robert Mahon working on the same project at the time of their deaths?"

"Dr. Mahon, the accident? Yes, they both were on the team working on LONG REACH. Surely you don't think there's any connection? Way back there..."

"It is a coincidence, don't you think, Dr. Dessel? Both on the same project. Both dead. And with them at the time of their deaths was the same woman."

"Dawna?"

"Yes, you know her?"

"Yes, it's a small town, and our scientific community is smaller still. We have parties, socialize."

Mark nodded. "Dr. Dessel. I would suggest that you double your guards, increase your security and your locked file checks, and put all of your guards on alert for at least a week. We'll see if we can contain this situation."

"The FBI didn't seem overly concerned."

"Did you tell them what LONG REACH is, and about the two dead men and the coincidence and the girl?"

"No."

"Then perhaps they don't have a need to know. You can use your own authority to beef up your security. I'd like to look at that explosion site later. Was it plastique?"

"Yes, we know that for sure. But all the other physical evidence has vanished, vaporized."

Mark stood to go. "Oh, these FBI people, are they on the site?"

"Yes, I've made an office available for them to use, and they have a pool secretary for any reports. I'll take you down there and introduce you."

A dozen offices down the hall, Dr. Dessel opened a door and let Mark into a double-sized office with three desks. Two men sat there, looking bored.

"Gentlemen, a compatriot of yours. This is Keith Zilke of the U.S. Justice Department. He's on this, too. I told him he could share facilities here if he needs them."

Dr. Dessel introduced him to Pete Sanchez, a slender Mexican-American with a trimmed moustache and friendly black eyes. He grinned and waved, then came over and shook hands. "Not sure why we're here, but when the Bureau says go . . . I'm from the Santa Fe office."

The second man, Howard Goodman, was five-foot-nine, 35 pounds overweight at 175, blond with blue eyes and light skin. He waved from where he sat. "Yeah, yeah. We won't give you no shit, Zilke. This is a damn dead end anyway. No way in little green hell we gonna ever find the nut who planted that bomb! We should go home and work on something important."

Mark had narrowed his eyes slightly as Goodman waved. It was the same man, the FBI nut who had sworn out vengeance on the Penetrator, and for several years had been on a one-man crusade with a free rein to bring in the Penetrator. He had missed. What was he doing here? Reassigned?

Mark frowned. "Goodman, Goodman, Howard Goodman. Weren't you on some kind of a special assignment for a while?"

"Goddamn, I'm famous! See. Sanchez, you chili pepper! I told you I was fucking famous! Yeah,

Zilke, I been working on this bastard the Penetrator, trying to track down his ass and sling it into some Fed slammer where he won't never see light again."

"Who?"

"The Penetrator . . . What the hell, forget it. I got to get out of this asshole of New Mexico and back to work. I can't function out here. I don't even have a twenty-four hour crime wire. I might as well be fishing in the Rockies, for all the damn good I'm doing."

Dr. Dessel waved and closed the door as he left.

Howard Goodman didn't notice him leave. "I'll tell you what the fuck I'm going to do. I'm going to call D.C. right now and get the assistant director's big hairy ear and give him the word. I just ain't going to sit still for this reassignment crap. Know what I mean? I've got me a Penetrator to find. The director himself put me on that special detail. So I didn't quite get him in the time limit. I know more now than any man alive about this Penetrator bastard—where he goes, what he does, how he makes his contacts, how he makes law enforcement agencies look bad."

Sanchez began to laugh. "Goodman, go chase a gopher, will you? You've been bitching about this assignment all day. Besides, maybe Zilke here can do us some good. Zilke, you know anything we don't? Can we make any swaps with you on information?"

Mark laughed, "First, I'd have to know what you know, and you haven't told me that yet. Hey, they have any coffee around here? I think I can buy for everybody and invest an hour or so with a couple of Bureau men without hurting my image too much."

Chapter 6

OVER THE DAMN FENCE!

It was ten o'clock the following morning before Joanna had all of the environmentalists fed. She discovered that the newest member of the organization automatically became the cook, and at this site, that meant making sandwiches and buying milk. All but two of the group drank milk, which surprised Joanna. Some of them also were borderline health food freaks, which was not surprising. She wiped her hair off her forehead and closed the mayonnaise jar. It should last two days in the warm weather—but the jar would be empty long before that.

Joanna grinned thinking about the night before. She had brought in the groceries and found Clutch waiting for her. They put the food in the kitchen, and Clutch moved in on her fast. She had pushed him away and was about ready to use some karate defensive tactics when she changed her mind and laughed instead.

"Hey, black man. You think this is your own private harem around here or something?"

"Damn right." He pushed her against the sink, and his mouth came down on one of her breasts, gently biting through the T-shirt.

"Get off me, you black bastard!" she said sharply. "That sort of jive disgusts me. Don't you know I'm gay?"

He jumped back at once. "You're gay?"

"Damn right, so get your shitty man-hands off me!"

"I don't believe it, white girl!"

"Go ask H. R. Why do you suppose I'm in this dump, just to get some free pot or maybe some coke? No way. And I'm sure as hell not here as some ridiculous bleeding heart to save the environment. I got something else in mind. Just like you got something else in mind. This is all a smokescreen for you."

He stared at her, his large eyes mostly white for a moment in his black face. Then he shrugged.

"Yeah, I guess it could be, you're here for H. R.'s pussy." He picked up the candle. "Yeah, I see how it could figure. Okay, honkey tight-twat, you got your way tonight. Tomorrow I'm having a little talk with H. R."

Joanna grinned thinking about it. She had maintained her cover and put down big Clutch Washington at the same time. That had been half the fun. But tonight it would be different. Before noon the word would be out on her.

The more talk she heard around the house, the more convinced she was that Western Naturalists United was somehow mixed up with a plot to stop the big weapons project at the Labs, just as H. R. Rivers had said that first night. But how?

They had an eleven-o'clock meeting around the fireplace. A small teepee fire burned, even though it was warm in the house. Rivers stood against the stones watching the blaze. Today she wore a T-shirt and her jeans with knee-high boots. Her small breasts barely made a dent in the T-shirt. When the group quieted, she turned and glared at them.

"You got no damn dedication!" She let that sink

into their minds as the 20 young people watched her. Most of them were caught up by the statement. "Most of you people wouldn't know how to stage a good demonstration or to pick a real fight if we had one. Well, I've got news for you. Tonight we take some action, we take some chances, and we put it on the line. Anybody going to shit out on me, do it tonight. As soon as it gets dark, we let those bastards on the other side of the fence know that we're here and we're mad as hell. We'll show them that the people in this country have the power!"

"Power to the people! Power to the people!" The group picked up the chant and Joanna joined in. She realized that Clutch was the one who initiated it; evidently he was the one to start the spontaneous chanting.

She waved at them and they stopped.

"Tonight we're going to hit the Scientific Labs. I don't know just what we'll do. It depends what they do. Clutch, I want you to bring one two-stick charge with you and a thirty-second fuse. No, bring two charges. This will be a probe to test their defenses. Tonight we'll see how dedicated we are, and how insistent they are."

She paused, put a small stick on the fire, then turned back to them. "Any of you ever been in the military service?"

Four hands went up, three men and one girl.

"Good. Tonight we might take some casualties, but we'll be ready for it." She looked around the group. "Martha, why are we here?"

A girl of 20 stood. She was about six months pregnant, and smiling past long, dirty blonde hair.

"We're here because we're soldiers, and we're deeply committed to fight for the environment and not to let people know that we are mad as hell. We're ready to go into battle for our God-given natural land and air."

"Right, Martha. Thank you. We're an army, and we won't let the industrial-government conspiracy go any farther. Government helps develop these products that rape the land and poison our children, that irradiate our food and our whole land. We've got to put a stop to this government pollution, this genocide by edict, this mass poisoning by subterfuge and food additives, stop high radiation release and the strontium-ninety fallout."

"Power to the people," Clutch began. She let the phrase be chanted two dozen times before she held up her hand to quiet them.

"Right on! Now, I don't want anyone stoned tonight for our hit. So smoke your grass early, and let's be alert and ready to follow instructions. You three men who had military training, I want you as my squad leaders. Break our group into three squads. I'll give you instructions later on. As soon as it gets dark, we'll move out, so get some sleep this afternoon." She turned and walked away. The members stood, talking excitedly about the upcoming strike.

Rivers looked at Joanna and motioned for her. Joanna walked up to the leader and smiled.

"Right on, sister. You really laid it on the line for all of us. What are we after tonight?"

Ms. Rivers smiled. "You'll find out tonight, Melis. Right now we need to talk." She turned and walked to her first-floor room and went inside, leaving the door open. Joanna followed. As soon as she was inside, Rivers closed the door and leaned against it.

Her smile was more open now, she had relaxed, her performance was over and part of her mask slipped..

"I wasn't sure about you before, Melis, but I'm glad."

"Oh, I really want to help, H. R. I mean, the Western Naturalists United are doing a great job. You get more headlines than the Sierra Club, and you make a lot of sense. Think of the factories that have been cleaned up just because you wrote them a letter and threatened to picket and sent pictures to the TV news programs."

"Yes, true, Melis. True. But that's not what I'm talking about." She rubbed her hand slowly across her face, then she looked straight at Joanna, a stare so frank and open that it was emotionally expensive. "I want to talk about you, Melis. Clutch told me you put him down last night. I like that." She moved toward Joanna. "I like you, Melis. I did from the first time I saw you. You're the kind of girl I really go for. I fell in love with you that very first day, Melissa."

Joanna tried not to show surprise. She walked to the window and looked into the weed-filled back yard. Was this moving in the direction she was afraid it was?

"No, Melis, you don't have to say anything. I don't even know how far you are into this. I mean you're no hardened butch dyke, and I like that. But I don't know if you're out of the closet or still showing a straight side." H. R. Rivers stripped her own T-shirt off over her head.

Joanna stared at the small girl's slender, naked torso, and at the tiny breasts. Rivers walked toward her.

"Melis, darling, I'm not like the other girls you've

had. I'm always soft and gentle. Just because I don't have tits doesn't mean a thing. We both know that's not the important part. And, sweetheart, I know some tricks that will leave you gasping in thrills you've never known before. We've got plenty of time, we'll just go slow and easy."

She stood beside Joanna and smiled, touched her cheek, reached up and kissed her lips, then put her arm around Joanna's shoulder and with her other hand brushed Joanna's breasts.

At once Joanna stepped away, shrugging off the arm, moving out of physical contact.

"I'm sorry, H. R., I didn't know." She looked frankly at the leader. "I'm not really gay. Last night I was afraid of Clutch. He's so big and looked mean and he's black. I'm no prude, but I've never made it with a black man, and I was so frightened, I didn't know what else would stop him."

Rivers stared at her, her smile fading, a look of regret and pain and frustration replacing it. "But . . . Melissa. Have you even tried a girl? You might be gay and not even know it."

Joanna felt the intensity behind the woman's eyes, the desire, the power. Slowly Joanna shook her head.

"No, Rivers, I don't think so. I like men. No hard feelings?"

H. R. Rivers turned and put on her T-shirt. She didn't say a word. Joanna saw the hurt in the other woman's face and wanted to explain that it was nothing personal, but she knew at once that nothing she said would help. So Joanna walked out of the room. As she did, she felt a new vibration, a new threat that was hanging over her head. She had no way of knowing how Rivers would react to rejection. But Joanna told herself that she would be doubly cautious from now on.

Joanna didn't see the leader for the rest of the afternoon. When it came time for the second and last meal of the day, they had soup. Someone had stolen a two-burner propane camp stove complete with fuel bottles. Joanna bought a cooking pot at the hardware store and spoons and bowls. The soup was from a gallon can of dry mix and was delicious.

Clutch took a bowl in to Ms. Rivers, and Joanna was beginning to feel a little better. She was inside the group, she had put down Clutch with the gay bit and then rejected Rivers because she was straight. She guessed that Rivers wouldn't let anyone in the group know that Joanna had rejected their leader.

Clutch came back for another bowl of soup and shook his head.

"What a damn waste of a knockout of a woman!" he said softly to her as he filled his bowl.

"Hey, hot shot. What's a dander for the old gander might be loose for the goose, know what I mean?" He nodded and moved on.

As soon as it was dark, Joanna went with the others toward the Labs gate. They drove a few blocks and left the three cars, then filtered along the street to the fence. They had three squads, and the leaders conferred in the dark.

H. R. Rivers came up to Joanna and pushed something into her hand. It was a revolver.

"Ever used one of these?" Rivers asked.

"Yes. My father taught me how to shoot."

"Good. If any of those sons of bitches out there fire at us, we shoot back."

Joanna wished she could see the woman's face, but she turned in the darkness and was gone. Automatically, Joanna checked the rounds in the piece. It felt like a .38 and had about a 2-inch barrel. There were six rounds—she could see the lead slugs in the moonlight. Joanna had been hoping the piece had blanks.

The plan was simple. Three men would form a pyramid, boosting a fourth man onto the top of the barbed wire of the 8-foot protective border fence. The top man wore a heavy padded jacket and would lie across the wire. The others would climb up the human ladder, roll over the man on the barbed wire and be in the facility.

It almost worked. The man mashing down the barbed wire on top tripped an alarm wire, and a siren wailed in the distance. Nearby, a pair of floodlights came on, turning a 50-yard section of the perimeter fence into daylight. The second squad leader, a wiry young man of about 20, called Charro, jumped up the pyramid and tried to get over the fence. But he slipped, the pyramid faltered and fell, and the other two on top crashed down beside them.

The sirens continued to sound.

Before they could reposition the pyramid, a jeep slammed into the lighted zone and slid to a stop 10 feet from the wire and across from the demonstrators. Even before it stopped, a loudspeaker blared from the rig.

"This is an area restricted by the United States government. We are authorized armed guards. Disengage yourself from the fence and fall back to the road. You are trespassing, and we will enforce our orders to prevent any and all nonauthorized personnel from entering this facility. We will use force of arms if needed."

Three guards leaped out of the jeep. All carried automatics. They stood at the fence with their weapons at the ready but not aimed. The voice came from the jeep loudspeaker.

"I say again, retreat from the fence. This section is wired with a 440-volt charge, and the switch to activate that power will be thrown in thirty seconds. You have thirty seconds to disengage yourselves from the barrier fence, or you will be electrocuted where you stand."

The group members near the wire looked at the rest of the protestors, waiting their orders. There came a shrill scream from one of the girls. The men pulled away from the fence, dropped to the ground, and moved out of the light. As they pulled back, a two-stick dynamite explosion 50 yards to the left and out of the lighted section blasted through the still night air with the shock of an earthquake. Part of the fence twisted, broke, and curled back from the force of the powder. More lights snapped on, showing a gaping hole in the fence. One of the guards turned and fired three rounds into the fence near the hole.

The sound of the gunfire was contagious. A dozen rounds came from the protestors' handguns. By this time, all 20 had faded away out of the lighted zone and fallen into whatever kind of cover they could find—behind trees, in ditches, or flat on the ground. None of the rounds they fired seemed to hit the guards across the fence, who scurried behind the jeep for protection.

"Cease fire, cease fire!" the loudspeaker voice came from the jeep speaker. "There will be no more firing!"

Two more jeeps screamed into the area, and a

dozen men with pistols at the ready ringed the far side of the fence. The explosion had torn a man-sized hole in the heavy steel fence. One of the jeeps was driven into the hole, blocking it.

The whispered word went around the protest group hiding in the dark. "Cease fire and pull out." They did, vanishing into the darkness and assembling back at the cars.

"Is anyone hurt?" Rivers asked. No one complained. "Squad leaders, count your people. Make sure everyone is here."

Ten minutes later, they were back in the old house, lighting the candles. Rivers collected the weapons and noticed that Joanna had fired two rounds. She nodded and turned away. Joanna had fired twice in the air when the others fired. Now she was glad that she had.

"We'll have an evaluation tomorrow at ten," Rivers said, then went into her room and closed the door.

Tabler watched her go. The leader must be pleased. For her, it had been a successful attack. The guards had been faked into firing, there was an explosion that ripped the fence open, and the facility's full contingent of guards must have been called out. Rivers had learned a lot about the Labs with one small move. And the demonstrators had fired guns at the guards. Handguns, but the guards probably wouldn't know that. Demonstrators who fired guns were something new. Most of those men probably had never been shot at before.

Tabler was exhausted. She didn't like undercover jobs, and this one probably was unimportant—unless it really was tied in with that monster weapon that evidently was being researched and developed here. Still, she didn't see how she was going to help much tagging this outfit.

She went up to her room, moved her sleeping bag to the far corner of the area and, without taking off her clothes, climbed inside and zipped the bag up tight.

No one bothered her all night. She woke up twice to find candles burning. Across the room she saw naked bodies entwined in some of the strangest coupling positions she had ever heard about. Sleepily, she decided she'd have to try them sometime . . . sometime.

Chapter 7

THE BARE BETATRON FACTS

The Penetrator spent a frustrating night trying to get into the house where the suicide took place. When the sheriff's car finally left, the woman came back and stayed, with all lights on and all radios and TVs in the house blaring. At two o'clock A.M., she was still up and, from what he could see, drinking heavily. He went back to the Plaza motel and used Tabler's bed.

Mark was pleased when he got to the Labs shortly after nine o'clock the next morning and the guard told him he was wanted in the director's office as soon as he arrived. It turned out to be a full-scale briefing on the LONG REACH program for the three federal law officers.

"Frankly, gentlemen, the attack last night by this group of environmental freaks has me worried," Dr. Dessel said. "I'm taking a whole new slant on this and I want—in fact, I urge you all—to give me all the support, help, advice, and suggestions that you can. Outside of a company of U.S. combat Marines, I have few ideas about what we can do."

They talked for ten minutes about security, and at last decided to ask for a platoon of about 40 men from the nearest military base to come to their assistance as guards. They would be on site at least until the environmentalists left.

"Gentlemen, I'm going to give you a detailed

briefing about our project and program. I've given you all a Need-to-Know clearance." He moved to a large flip chart and turned over the first blank page. The word *laser* appeared.

"Let me make this clear. We're not talking about the current science-fiction faddish use of laser beams. As you know, a laser is an acronym and means 'Light Amplification by Stimulated Emissions of Radiation.' This is a device that uses the natural oscillations of atoms or molecules between energy levels for generating coherent electromagnetic radiation in the ultraviolet, visible, or infrared regions of the spectrum.

"With our current technology and thinking, the laser is a limited-range weapon. What we're talking about is something far more complex, intricate, expensive, and effective. Operation LONG REACH is simply that: a long-range beam that can be useful in a number of ways.

"The laser is great at short ranges, say up to a mile. But even at that short distance, you need several beams focused on one target. The high-energy laser will produce an explosive flash when it hits a target. The TV shows are certainly right on that score, but they don't show you the fiery plume that also shoots backward from the target. In solid material a laser hit leaves a gaping hole as the target matter is instantly changed into plasma.

"What we are talking about now is a charged particle beam. This is not a laser. It's a real ray gun, if you will. These charged particles are atomic particles, which might be protons, neutrons, or electrons. This ray, or beam, is simply a stream of these charged particles propelled at a tremendous speed.

beam before we did, so we can only assume that they are ahead of us on it. We have made no dramatic breakthroughs, found no short cuts."

"And could Russian agents be trying to slow or stop your work here?" Sanchez asked.

"Yes, that's entirely possible. The CIA has informed me that this is a very real possibility."

"How would this gadget work in space? How would you pick up targets?" Goodman asked.

"That's not my part of the work; however, I assume some type of radar scan from the satellite, relayed to earth with built-in recognition for known satellites orbiting, and all the space junk up there, would be used. It would take close cooperation by anyone with a vehicle in space, so recognition could be built in and the benign craft not shot down accidentally. Once a real target was confirmed, the beams would be radar aimed, coordinated, locked in, and the rays fired, destroying the target."

He looked at the three men and when he heard no more questions, he continued.

"Gentlemen, this afternoon at one o'clock P.M., we hope to have a test firing of the device. It will be from a mobile truck in our back country range. It's still on the reservation and perfectly safe. This is not our first try, but it is an important step, and if it is successful it will mean that we have been able to contain the beam's spread and can now keep it in a tight, narrow configuration."

"Can we watch the test?" Sanchez asked.

Dr. Dessel frowned. "No, I'm afraid not. It would serve no purpose. I have a time study problem here, and it would seem obvious that your job is to curtail, arrest, stop, or otherwise prevent this radical group of ecology nuts from interfering with our top-secret work on this base. That, gentlemen, is your primary duty here, and I suggest that the three of you coordinate your actions, or get advice from your superiors about what action you should take. After the attack last night, and the gunfire, I can now file attempted murder charges on everyone you can identify who was at that fence. Add to that the destruction of government property, shooting into a top-secret base, attacking a U.S. facility, conspiracy, and probably a dozen other charges. Why don't you get out of here and arrest this H. R. Rivers woman and her gang? Almost anyone in town can show you the house on Ivy Street where they are camping out. First try to have them evicted, then arrested. You can hold them all on a conspiracy charge for two or three days."

"Hasn't your sheriff here made any arrests yet?" Sanchez asked.

"He usually lets you boys handle anything that gets out of whack here on the site. Now, if you'll excuse me, I have to get ready for the shot this afternoon. If you have any questions or problems, leave word with my secretary."

They had been dismissed. They got up and walked back to their office.

"Shit, I guess we should call D.C. and see what they want us to do on this thing," Goodman said.

"Right," Mark agreed. "I better check in, too. I'm basically an observer here, you understand that, so I don't want to get in your way."

Sanchez waved. Goodman belched and swore as they headed for their office and the phone. Mark faded away from them, put on his badge, and moved with purpose toward the garages where he had seen the big flatbed trucks the day before.

Dessel said they moved by truck. Anything that big meant big trucks and lots of them.

Mark found a bathroom and quickly slipped out of his coat and vest and changed into a set of blue coveralls like those the workmen wore in the facility garage. He had figured he'd use them as a cover so he could do some plain-sight snooping. This was a perfect set-up for him. He put on a bill cap with the word "FORD" printed across the front, and hid the briefcase where he could find it. Then he approached the lead man in the garage.

It took Mark five minutes to convince the man he was legitimate and wasn't trying to pull anything. He showed him his DOJ field agent I.D. and his clearances. He said he only wanted to surprise Dr. Dessel and go to the test as a worker rather than an observer. He had a three-axle license for California, and could handle one of the tractor trailer rigs if he needed to. The capper was a crisp, new $50 bill that Mark passed to the man, and he was given a berth as an assistant driver on one of the big 40-tire flatbeds. Two had already been loaded and driven away at 10 miles an hour. Two more would come after at a fast 12 miles an hour. They had a 10 mile trip, and then it would take at least two hours to set up.

Mark talked little with the driver as they moved away from the central garage area. The tractor picked up an overwidth 40-foot utility trailer and powered away with it in low gear.

The driver was grousing about the time, saying they should have left with this load a half-hour ago. They stopped on a small, flat hilltop that had been bulldozed down some years ago to provide a firm platform about the size of a football field. The trucks pulled up in preassigned places, and 50 technicians went to work. Mark lounged with the other drivers, watching. A game of cribbage at a penny a point began, and Mark moved off for a better look at the production taking place in front of him.

There were four low-boy trailers, each loaded heavily with some type of large equipment mounted on wheels and with breakaway box sides that came off. Large electric generators were started up and geared into full production, then idled down. Huge electric cables were strung everywhere. They were 2 inches in diameter and every 10 feet had a red and white sign that said, "Do not crush, do not run over with a vehicle!"

At the brow of the hill, another truck trailer was parked, on this one the entry side rolled up and vanished into the overhead like a sliding door. Before he could get closer to it, somebody shouted at him.

"Hey, driver. Dammit, get back where you belong."

Mark turned back toward the big trucks and saw two Ford Fiestas arrive. Six men got out of each one and went to the lead trailer at the edge of the hill.

After that Mark wasn't sure what happened. Another side came off the lead trailer, and three men in white coats moved around the massive equipment there. Four large TV monitors, 6 feet square, were set up and shaded from the sun in shadow boxes so they could get a picture.

Several 30-power scopes were positioned around the rim of the hill. The men in the white coats made what Mark guessed were final adjustments to the machine, then went to the scopes. In another truck, linked by a dozen of the big electrical cables, a man who must have been the project director stood before a panel. He sighted through some kind of device, and on the hill, part of the huge equipment rotated slowly a foot, then elevated a few inches.

A loudspeaker cut in. "Power Supply ready."

Another voice: "Target positioned and ready."

Other voices chimed in on the checklist.

"Target area cleared of all personnel."

"Target area loudspeakers activated, warnings being given continually."

"Beta ready for activation."

"Power supply at proper voltage and constant."

"Activate betatron."

Several seconds went by.

"We have velocity."

A few more seconds.

"We have acceptable voltage."

At once a voice crashed over the end of the sentence.

"FIRE! FIRE! FIRE!"

Mark watched the big trailer at the edge of the dropoff, but he heard no report, saw nothing move. He heard a cheer and noticed that everyone else was watching the shielded TV monitors. He ran for a better view. Dimly he saw the picture of a cow standing on a barren hillside, chained to a post driven into the ground.

The cow stood there munching one moment, the next she simply melted to the ground, her legs falling apart. Her head and neck detached from her body and fell to the ground. A gush of steam came from the carcass. The camera zoomed in, and as the rib cage hit the ground, it split open and Mark could see what looked like a huge slab of well-done roast beef, steaming and smoking in the sunshine.

The cheers from the men on the hill sounded

again and again. There was an instant replay as the cow came apart and Mark watched it.

The loudspeakers boomed.

"Congratulations, team! A precise hit within five centimeters of dead center target position. A fantastic shot! The best ever in our testing from a one-mile range. The subject animal is now one huge chunk of roast beef if anyone is hungry enough."

Another cheer went up from the technicians.

When the P.A. voice came back, it was all business again.

"Prepare second target area."

"Second target in place, and ready. All personnel cleared. Bungs have been left out of all three barrels. A-OK here."

The procedure was followed as before, and Mark saw the huge machine on the truck move again, this time rotating 15 degrees or more and depressing several degrees. They were aiming the betatron, if he remembered what he had heard this morning.

"We have acceptable particle voltage," the impersonal loudspeaker voice said.

"FIRE. FIRE. FIRE."

This time Mark had been watching the screen and saw a stack of 55-gallon gasoline drums on the barren hillside. One moment they were there, the next instant the whole frame filled with an explosion that drenched the area with burning gasoline.

The cheers were continuous. At last the speaker broke in.

"Congratulations again, crew. This hit was a little sloppy. We were three centimeters off dead center at three-quarters of a mile. As expected, the intense heat generated by the particle beam vaporized enough of the flammable liquid to act as a detonator, which in turn exploded and turned the three barrels of gasoline into one giant Molotov cocktail. Now for the third and toughest test. Prepare the five-mile range test."

It took longer this time, then after about 20 minutes, the loudspeakers gave the word.

"Five-mile test target area reports all ready. Target in place and set precisely by laser alignment. All personnel are cleared from the two-mile safety zone. Warning loudspeakers are continuous. Five-mile target area now ready."

Mark saw it come on the screen. There was nothing but a dug-out spot of ground in front of a small hill. In the center of the cleared spot, three apple-box sized cardboard containers had been stacked, one on top of the other.

The fire command came and Mark watched the screen. Nothing happened. Then slowly smoke came from the corner of one of the boxes, and soon the whole box was burning. There was no explosion. The camera zoomed in, and the cardboard had flaked away. Mark could see that the slender sticks inside the top box were burning. Dynamite! They had three cases of dynamite, and it was all burning.

The picture held as the P.A. came on. "Two out of three isn't bad. Our hit on the dynamite boxes, due to the laser alignment was four millimeters off perfect center! Nothing is wrong with our aim, or our beam spread. Now I'm told that our modern dynamite is so stable that it can be shot with a .45 slug, thrown out of an airplane and land on cement or burned as you see now, without exploding. So I'd say we have three for three. Not bad for anybody coming up to bat in this league. That's it for today. Let's pack it up and get out of here."

Chapter 8

THREE SHOTS TO BLOTTO

Mark walked into the lawmen's room at the Labs headquarters about four o'clock P.M. after he got back from the test shot. He was dressed again in his three-piece suit and carried the briefcase.

"Where the hell you been?" Goodman asked. "We was thinking of getting up a little poker game."

"Had to check out something about that ecology nut, Rivers, but I didn't get very far."

"Hell, you won't get anywhere with her. She's a gay bitch with no tits, no ass, and no brains," Goodman said.

"So what else is happening? Get a line on anyone who might be behind all this?" Mark asked.

Goodman was indignant, "You expect me to work on this son of a bitch of an assignment? Not me. It's a dead end. I might as well be picking lint out of my asshole for all the good I'm doing here. All of us for that matter. If I was back in D.C., I could dig into my Penetrator files. Now *there's* something worthwhile. I only brought one briefcase full of Penetrator records with me, and that's not enough to get a good start."

"Your what file?" Mark asked. "You mentioned something about that the other day."

Goodman shook his head in disbelief. "Zilke, where the hell you been living the last few years, in a deep hole somewhere? This is just the biggest damn wanted bastard we've got in our whole fucking files. He's wanted in thirty to thirty-five states now for everything from mass murder to arson, mayhem, kidnapping, and illegal flight. We've got so much paper on this dude, you wouldn't believe it. Thinks he's a damn one-man army of some kind. A do-gooder who shoots his way out of trouble."

"He's wanted in thirty-five states? You've got to be kidding," Mark said, trying hard not to laugh at Goodman's frustration.

"Hell no, I ain't kidding. Claims he's a crime fighter, that he hits only the bad guys, the crooks, the villians, the Mafia and organized crime goons. I admit he does some of that, but the lousy newspapers give him so much ink, they've made him into some kind of a bastard folk hero. Some of them even claim he's a modern-day Robin Hood."

"And you say he's been getting away with it for years?"

"Yeah, far too long. He's just a damned mercenary. He takes whichever job pays the most. I know for a fact that he's gotten away with more than a million dollars in cold cash this past year. And you think that gun-happy bastard pays any income tax? Hell no. He works for the highest buck. Now, some people, even some jerks in our own outfit, say fine. Let him wipe out the whole damn mess of Mafia, the Syndicate, organized crime, and spies and all them jerkoffs. But that just won't work. What says this gunslinger won't turn around and accept his next job from the ever-loving Mafia? Then what? Instead of some coke pusher he goes after a mayor or a U.S. senator, maybe even the president himself! This bastard is good, I'll give him that. But what happens when the big money is on the other side?

Shit, you know what'll happen. This Penetrator will shift gears and sides so fast, it'll twist your bow tie into a granny!"

Mark laughed, sipped at the coffee, and put his feet up on the desk. "Goodman, we never hear much about him in Justice. But from what you say, it sure doesn't sound like you're making much progress in your crusade against this guy. You've got the whole resources, the guns, the power of the Bureau. Why can't you tree one lone gun toter out there?"

"Lucky. He's been stupid-assed lucky. Don't ask me why. I've had this guy close to trapped, and then he vanishes on me. Once some damned civilian helped him get away when I had him cold. And another time I missed him by about twenty seconds. He was going down when I was going up. His luck can't hold out forever. I'll get him. I'll stuff his ass in the slammer for a hundred and fifty years for openers and then I'll go down every visiting day and spit in his face."

"That's what we need more of," Mark said chuckling. "Law officers with a cool, objective viewpoint." He looked at Sanchez. "Is the whole bureau this gung-ho on tracking down the Penetrator?"

"Not me, man. He's done a number on a batch of coyotes running illegals into this country. He burned the coyotes good and didn't touch the Mexicans. Helped them in fact. And then he put down a big heroin connection out in L.A. I like what he's doing, and he's going into the heart of some of our problems."

"The heart?" Goodman asked exploding. "He leaves a trail of bodies and burned buildings wherever he goes. And he always comes out of it with a bundle of cash. If there's no cash in it, he never shows up."

Sanchez grinned at Mark, "My man Goodman here is the Bureau nut on the Penetrator. I'd just as soon let him have his head, do what he wants to do out there. I've heard this Penetrator never shoots at an honest cop. Course he did take out a few of the crooked cops in Seattle, but no law officer has to be afraid of this guy. And sometimes he moves in and does some of our work for us. He jumps on guys we can't touch legally, but who are dirty as hell and everybody knows it. This Penetrator cat charges in with his .45 in one hand and some dynamite in the other and brings justice without due process. Now that is something every cop wishes that he could do sometimes. Goodman is a little weird about this guy, but usually Goodman is halfway stable. His biggest trouble is he plays a lousy poker hand. Got some time?"

"Thanks but I never play. I used to have a problem with lady luck. It's like that first drink for an alcoholic."

"Oh, sorry. Forget I mentioned it."

"Find out anything more about this case?"

Sanchez shook his head. "Not one hell of a lot. Oh, we did get out of Dr. Dessel that this Dawna Lane has been around town for two or three years, and that she's been in the social circle with the Labs management people and scientists. She was the cause of another man lost on this same project eight or ten months ago. She had an affair with one of the top scientists on the program. His wife found out about it and divorced the guy the next day. This scientist just kind of folded, couldn't take the gossip, and quit the program and went back to teaching at some little college."

"Sweet little Dawna Lane, she must be quite a girl," Mark said. An uneasiness began working through him. She was along when two men on the program died, and a third one quit because of her. Mark waved at the other two.

"Well, stay cool, I've got to pick up some cleaning, or they'll throw it out."

He went to his car and drove away, wondering more and more about Dawna Lane. Why not just go over and see her? It was 4:30; she might be home.

Mark drove past the house once, came back, and stopped across the street. She answered his second knock. He didn't expect her to be dressed in mourning and she wasn't.

Dawna wore a tight green sweater and matching slacks. She looked sleek and smooth, as though she was just ready to go out. The woman smiled at him, and he guessed she was about 23.

"I bet you're a cop, right? And I don't even care. You're the cutest one I've seen here so far. What did I do now?"

"Miss Lane?"

"Right, Dawna Lane."

"I'm Keith Zilke with the Justice Department." He flipped his fake badge showing her his buzzer, and she glanced at it for a minute. "There are a few questions..."

"A few more, right? Damn. I bet I've answered a good thousand questions in the past day-and-a-half."

He liked her green almond-shaped eyes and small nose. She wasn't beautiful, more cute, and she had a sleek, trim figure showing through the tight green sweater and pants.

"This has got to be a record for me. I've never flirted with so many cops in my life; sheriff deputies, the sheriff himself, the FBI men, plant security, and now the damn Justice Department. Wow! Hey what's keeping the state cops and the C.I.A.?" She grinned, and Mark took an immediate liking to this girl, the one he figured had already killed two men.

"Can we talk a minute?"

"Oh, sure, come on in. Pardon me if I was staring. I think it's those gorgeous black eyes of yours that did me in. They are simply fantastic."

They went into the house. It was furnished well without being overdone. The chairs and couch were good quality. Two oil paintings hung on one wall. A TV and long stereo console sat waiting.

"Frankly, Miss Lane, we in Justice are concerned with another aspect of this problem at the Labs. We're a bit worried about this band of ecology freaks who shot up the place recently. And now two men are dead who were working on the program. We are led to believe that there must be some kind of foreign influence here, some harrassment, some threat. Most of the people on the program are stable and well adjusted. A man like Stanley Duyck doesn't just blow out his brains unless someone is putting a lot of pressure on him. And I'd like to find out who and what and why."

She sat down and motioned for him to do the same. The woman blinked rapidly, and her face worked for a moment, but she caught control just in time and did not cry.

"What I'm saying is that I'd like you to think back, Miss Lane, and see if you can remember anything either man said about being pressured, offered bribes, threatened, even any communication with anyone outside the Labs about his work there."

She looked at Mark openly. "Damn. I don't remember a thing. And this isn't just off the top of my head. I've been thinking about this angle ever since Stanley died. I was pretty broken up for a while." She looked up and Mark wondered at the real concern on her face. She was either telling the truth or a damn good actress.

"I can't think of a single time when Stanley ever said anything about any kind of spy or foreigner talking to him. There was no hint of anything like that. He did get moody, but you know all that. Sorry, that's about the best I can do."

"Well, I'm glad you had thought about it. But sometimes an outside contact might happen casually. For example, did he ever shut the door, keeping you out, when he made a phone call or when he got a call? Even one time?"

She sighed and it did interesting things to her sweater. "Yes, I've seen him close the door a few times. But he said it was just boring shop talk I wouldn't understand or be interested in and he needed the TV sound closed out. Are things like that what you're hunting?"

"Sure, yes, that's a start. If you don't have anything to do for a few minutes, I thought we might just talk. Maybe we'll come up with some more ideas and instances like that one—establish a kind of pattern."

"Damn, there was some good TV on this afternoon, too." She hesitated. "Hell, why not? I mean, if I can help in any way, I want to." She stretched and the sweater clung more tightly. "How about a cup of coffee? I just made a new pot."

"Yes, please, black."

She smiled at him. "I like those eyes. Damn, but you've got sexy eyes." She grinned and went into the kitchen. Mark watched the interesting wiggle of her tight slacks as she moved away.

"Miss Lane, have you lived around here long?"

"About three years, maybe a little more," she said from the kitchen. "I work part-time at a savings and loan, as a relief teller. It's not much, but it gives me something to do."

She came back with two mugs of coffee and handed him one. This time she sat on the sofa 3 feet from him.

"Now, I was trying to remember. Stanley was a good man, and I don't mean just in bed. He decorated this place after we moved in. He picked out the pictures, the furniture, even the goddamn drapes. He was a good all-around man."

Mark smiled and lifted the steaming coffee. He hoped the coffee would relax her more, and maybe she would slip up. He let the brew touch his lips and reacted at once. She was watching him.

"Hey! Wow that's hot. I'm not used to it so hot."

She laughed. "That's the only way I can drink it. I should have warned you."

"This will be fine, I'll let it cool off a little." Mark put the coffee down, and they talked for five minutes. She couldn't think of anything else that might tie down any kind of a foreign influence or contact. Mark had reacted to the coffee with more surprise than hurt. Through his keen senses, he could tell the cup was loaded with a not-too-sophisticated knock-out drop. Four or five swallows of that stuff, and he would pass out like a dumb drunk in a harem. She had been drinking her coffee. Now she rose, telling him about a picnic they took early in the summer.

"Oh, my cup ran dry. Yours should be cool enough. I'm going to get some more coffee. I'll bring in the pot."

As soon as she left the room, Mark poured almost all his coffee out on the rug at his end of the sofa where she couldn't see it. When she came back in, he was pretending to sip at the brew.

"This has finally cooled off to where I like it," he said. He kept the cup in his hand so she couldn't see how full it was. He waved her away with the pot. "Don't get this any hotter, or I'll be here till midnight."

They went on talking about everything and nothing. He told her that the smallest item might trigger something in her memory. He pretended to sip occasionally at the coffee, but never actually drank any. Soon he set the cup down, and it was almost empty.

"More coffee?" she asked.

"No, no more, thanks, I should be going. Oh, pardon me." He shook his head as if to clear it. "I'm a little woozy, I guess I didn't have much lunch." He started to stand and fell back on the sofa. "I can't figure . . . can't figure it out." Mark began blinking, rubbing his eyes and trying to stretch them open. "Don't understand . . . it . . . I feel . . . sort . . . of . . ." Then Mark's head fell against the back of the sofa, and his hand dropped to his lap.

Mark had faked the whole routine and steeled himself to withstand any test. He heard movement, but didn't open his eyes.

"Mr. Zilke." she said, her voice harder now. "Zilke, wake up. You can't sleep here."

He made no response. Mark felt her pick up his arm, which he had willed to be limp. She lifted it and dropped it in his lap. It fell like a hunk of granite.

Dawna grinned. She took a fingernail and scratched it along the soft skin under his eye. The eye twitched but remained closed. She used a pin from the nightstand and jammed it a quarter of an inch into Mark's thigh. He groaned but did not otherwise stir. It was a normal minimal reaction to pain in an unconscious state.

Dawna looked at Mark. "What a damn shame," she said softly. Then she went to the kitchen and made two phone calls. Mark could hear little of what she said. She was back a moment later, and he felt her hands on him. This time she took his billfold from his back pants pocket, and he guessed she was going through it.

"My, my, Keith. Aren't we the rich one? Five hundred and twenty dollars. I'll leave the twenty, so it won't look like you were robbed. Put it down as the price for the coffee." She giggled and her hand pushed the wallet back in his rear pocket. She patted down his front pockets, found his car keys, and took them out. Then her hand brushed his crotch. "Oh, Lordy, I bet you would have been dynamite in bed. I can tell."

She left him and he heard her walk out. Mark didn't stir.

Ten minutes later, the doorbell rang, and she let someone in. They talked in the hall quietly; then a person went outside and Mark heard a car drive in beside the house. They must be going to use a side door, he thought. Smart. The two of them carried Mark out the side door to the car. Mark risked a small peep out one eye when he was face down and saw that it was almost full dark now. They pushed and stuffed him in the back seat. The girl got out, and he heard only one front door open and then slam shut. Soon the car was moving.

He had no idea where they were going. It would be simple to kill the driver from behind, but the car might go out of control. He'd wait until they got wherever they were going before he made his move. That way he could be certain the girl wasn't along. He didn't have his .45. The girl had forgotten about searching his jacket, but the man with her hadn't and had found the weapon.

He opened his eyes and looked around. It probably was his own rented car. He could see the street lights flashing overhead, and now and then another car met them. Gradually the town noises vanished and then the overhead lights were gone too. They were in the country. The car worked up a hill, turned off on a gravel surface, and stopped. How convenient. A man drives over a cliff in a rented car. A tragic accident, but no one could be suspected. Mark heard the front door slam, then the rear one open. He was watching now, and had turned over on his back, his legs toward the driver's side door. Mark saw the hulking figure reach in.

"Come on, little buddy. Time to play like you're driving this heap." As he leaned in and reached for Mark's feet, Mark exploded his legs outward, concentrating on making his heels hit flesh first. They caught the man in the chest, and Mark heard two ribs crack and a scream of pain, disbelief, and despair follow. The man flew backwards on his back into the gravel.

Mark leaped out of the car before the man could get his gun. Mark kicked his hand away from the belt, stripped a .38 revolver out and held it on the man writhing on the ground. He was a big one, about six-foot-four and 240 pounds, Mark guessed.

"On your feet, twinkletoes," Mark snapped. "Now you can play like a driver."

The man didn't move. Mark kicked him sharply in the side near the broken ribs. The man screamed in pain.

"Okay, dammit. You busted my ribs."

"Tough. Who do you work for?"

"You know I'm not telling you that," the man said, getting to his knees, then standing as he held onto the car for support.

Mark rammed a karate blow into the goon's smashed ribs, and a gutteral roar of agony exploded from his lips. When the man quieted, he looked at Mark with complete hatred.

"If I tell you, what does it buy me?"

"Your life. If the information is good. Now talk."

"I don't know who hired me. The girl is the contact. She relays the orders, pays me off. That's all I know."

Mark considered it. Could be. The hood was in no condition to think up fancy lies. "What were your orders for me?"

"Over the cliff in your car. Five hundred feet to the rocks. I walk two miles down the road, where she picks me up in an hour."

"Good. Get in the car. I'll tell them you stole it, drove out here, then panicked when I had a gun.

You tried to get away but went over the side. They'll believe it."

"Shit no. Nobody'll believe it."

"Then tell me who your boss is, or I put .38 slugs in your kneecaps, then your elbows. You'll never walk again."

"Christ no! I told you all I know. I work for her."

"She's a messenger girl. I want her boss."

"I don't know. Only been here two months. I can't learn everything in two months."

The big man had stumbled against the car now, and he put out his hands to catch himself. His ribs were hurting like raw, searing lines of fire. His hands came near his belt, and he started to move back, then his hand darted to his belt for a hide-out gun. The small automatic came up suddenly, and Mark dodged and squeezed off three shots from the .38 so fast, they sounded like one explosion. The heavy man took all three slugs in the chest and went down like a sack of wet cement. He rolled over and stared up at Mark, then without a word, he died.

Mark took a deep breath and shook his head. He hadn't intended to kill the man, not until he made that move. Mark wiped his own prints off the .38-caliber weapon and dropped it beside the body. He found his own .45 in the front seat and left the .25 automatic in the dead man's hand. Then Mark got in the car and headed back to town.

He drove a few minutes, then decided he would check out Dawna's house again. He was half a block away when he saw a car come out of her garage and drive toward downtown. It looked as if she was alone. Mark had to decide whether to follow her or investigate the house. He chose the house. In the darkness he parked and walked back a half-block to her house, faded into the shrubs, and a moment later was at the back door. He opened the lock with his pen knife against the unprotected bolt. Inside he searched quickly but carefully. She would never know that he'd been there.

Mark found an envelope with his creased 500 dollars in it under some panties in her dresser. He left it there. He wanted her to feel secure. Mark searched for another half-hour, looking in all the old and new places, but found nothing to tie her in with any other person or group. She was either working on her own, or an excellently trained professional. At last he gave up and put his pocket flash away.

This trail was a dead end, at least for tonight.

Chapter 9

BURN A PRETTY FIRE

The same evening that Mark struck out at Dawna Lane's house, Joanna Tabler sat cross-legged on the dirty carpet in front of the fireplace in the old two-story house, listening to H. R. Rivers. All 20 of her followers were there, and tonight their leader seemed angrier than usual.

"It's not just that these sons of bitches are polluting your air and mine, messing up the water we all drink, and poisoning our food. No, now the goddamn government passes laws making it illegal to do anything else! Well, this is one time when the people are going to rise up and say 'Enough!' As that movie said, 'We're all mad as hell and we're not going to take it anymore!'"

Clutch grabbed the phrase and began chanting it, and quickly the others picked it up, and the old house rang with the slogan. Rivers smiled grimly, then held up her hand, and the chanting stopped at once.

"We sure as hell aren't going to take it anymore. This damned big-business/government monopoly has gone far enough. Now they aren't satisfied with a few nuclear power plants blowing up and getting ready to melt down, scattering radiation all over the country. No, now they want to invent some kind of a doomsday weapon that will actually radiate all of us from space! They're making a big cannon out there at the Labs that they want to put on a goddamn satellite and shoot at things. Say they aim it wrong and it wipes out Chicago. Big deal, they say. Overpopulation is one of our problems. Anyway, who will miss Chicago?

"I'll miss Chicago. Right now is the time we let them know what we want, what we demand. We're going out to that fence tonight, and the gate is going to come open and we're going to get inside. A few two-stick charges will open some eyes. And we've got four good, old-fashioned WP grenades that will burn the living shit out of anything touched.

"Power, my friends, power is the key. And that power must be with the people!"

"Power with the people, power with the people." The chant began spontaneously this time, and Clutch didn't have to lead them. They kept repeating it as they filed out of the house, jumped into the three cars, and roared off into the darkness of early evening.

As before, they left the cars before they got to the Labs gates. They moved singly or in pairs, without attracting attention.

The first anyone at the Labs knew about the wild night they were going to have was when a small fire broke out in the dry grass and shrubs along the border line fence. Quart cans of gasoline sparked the fires, set at hundred-yard intervals, and soon a long line of flames licked at the steel posts and brought out the fire trucks from the Labs and from the city of Los Alamos.

A small crowd gathered. Clumps of people here and there stood along the street as the trail of flames gushed into some larger shrubs and ate away at dry grass. Then the gates of the Labs swung open to let the two town fire trucks roll inside. As the big machines geared up and drove through the gates, 20 members of the Western Naturalists United surged along with them, knocked down the surprised guards, and spewed into the restricted grounds with guards running after them.

Not more than two minutes later, fresh fires sprouted, these in the first series of buildings nearest the gate. The fire trucks abandoned the creeping grass and shrubs fires and charged with sirens screaming to the buildings where fire fighters quickly contained the WP-lit fires before these could do much damage.

Before the last fire was out, an explosion rocked the grounds, as the first two-stick bomb went off under the corner of a small building. It was followed at one-minute intervals by three more of the small explosions, one inside a building where the bomb had been thrown through a window.

By this time the plant security chief, Wilbur Winslow, was on the scene. He ordered the fire trucks to pull back as he and his men made a quick inspection of the bombed buildings. He told them to close the gates so none of the perpetrators could get away, then let the firemen clean up the last of the smoldering embers and began a dragnet inside the Labs to ferret out the attackers.

"Get those lousy kids and handcuff them!" Winslow roared. "Every nonauthorized person inside the gates is under arrest. Nail them. Close the goddamn gate. Nail those bastards now!"

The guards gathered up the people. Most of them were the ecology students; a few were townspeople who had rushed inside to help fight the fires. The locals were quietly released and ushered out the gate.

An unused building was opened to use for a booking area, and the sheriff was called into the action. Twelve of the "outside agitators," as Winslow called them, were arrested and taken to county jail. One of them was Joanna Tabler.

The sheriff stared at the group in his drunk tank, which was the only area in the small jail large enough to hold them.

"I don't know what the hell you people are trying to prove, but one thing is certain, you won't prove it around here for a few weeks. This is a federal charge, and you won't get off easily. We'll take you out one at a time and book you and let you make a phone call, and that's it. The time is now just after ten P.M. We should be through with all of you by eleven. Any questions?"

H. R. Rivers screamed back at him. "You pig! You dirty, lying, filthy pig! You're the worst part of this whole governmental-economic conspiracy to delude the population. And don't worry about any overnight accommodations. Our lawyer is waiting in your lobby. If we're not out of this crackerbox jail in an hour, you and your whole goddamn county are in for one hell of a lot of legal trouble. Do you read me, you pig?"

Sheriff Logan glowered at her. He was not used to being scolded that way in his own jail. He turned and left, to the hoots and jeers of the prisoners.

Back in his office, Sheriff Logan punched an outside line and called the district attorney. "Get your ass down here, Charlie, we got ourselves one shit pot full of trouble." He listened a minute. "How the hell should I know how bad the trouble is? Get down here now. The fucking environmentalists have a lawyer here, and I want you here to watch the whole damn procedure. Somebody has to know what's going on here, and it should be you. And Johnson, you don't have to stop to put on your tie or three-piece suit or your hairpiece. Get down here now!"

As it worked out, by eleven P.M. the bail had been paid on all twelve of the ecology kids, and they were released from custody.

The next morning Mark went to see the leader of the WNU. He wanted to meet her, to get some idea how she might be involved, and to see if it could have any bearing on the top-secret project. He also wanted to check on Tabler. He hadn't heard from her for two days.

When Mark walked up the weed-bordered cement ribbon to the front door, he heard laughing and shouting inside the two-story house. His knock went unanswered. The door stood open, and when he heard a chanting, he paused. When it was over, he took a step inside and waited.

"Hello. Anybody home?"

A few seconds later, a tall black man came into the hall and stared at him. Mark grinned.

"I'll be damned, it is you, Clutch Washington. Somebody said you were in town. What's happening? You still play with the big, round ball?"

The black face broke into a smile, but then it faded and he shook his head.

"No, man. I'm out of the game. Too much static. You here on business?"

"I'd like to talk to Ms. Rivers."

"She's busy."

"Yeah, I heard the pep talk. Tell her I'll wait in my car. As soon as she's free, give me a yell."

"Yeah man, I will. And thanks."

"Thanks for what, Clutch?"

"For remembering my two good years. Most folks forget you in a rush."

"Hey, we remember. With a little luck, you could have been in the NBA for ten years."

"Thanks."

Fifteen minutes later, Clutch came bounding down the front wooden steps and waved at Mark, who sat on the fender of his rented Ford.

Mark had expected a private meeting, but all 20 of her followers remained sitting on the floor, where they had been for the rally. Rivers paced in front of them. When Mark came in, she snorted.

"You've got to be with the FBI, right?"

"No way. I'm Justice Department, field agent Keith Zilke." He showed her his badge.

"Jesus, a fake badge and all. I used to have one of those I used in the fourth grade. You're hot shit. Now what do you want? We're busy here."

"Just a little communication. You and your pack of animals here can do all the shouting and ranting and raving you want to. Scream, preach, cajole all over the place. But the second you jump over that line into illegal activities, as you did last night, we are coming down on you like a ten-ton steamroller with an upset stomach. We're hitting you with every felony charge we can, including arson, destruction of government property, transporting an explosive device onto a government installation, and bombing a government building. That's just for starters. There are five or six misdemeanors as well. You think you're smart and cool, don't you, Rivers? And the rest of you, you think she's going to be able to protect you when you get on that witness stand under charges? All twelve of you who got caught dirty-handed last night are in for a lot of trouble. Three to four felonies each. And that's hard time for five to ten for each felony. You kids could wind up in the slammer for twenty to thirty years! Think about that. What good can you do the environment locked behind prison walls somewhere? Think about it the next time some loudmouth tries to talk you into something that's stupid as well as being illegal."

"Are you through, you cretin with ears, you big shit mouth? Because if you don't think you are, you're wrong." She made a motion, and Clutch and three other big men from the group stood and moved behind Rivers.

"We aren't through with our work here, whatever-your-name was. And since we aren't through, we aren't leaving. Those charges you talked about are simply that, charges. Nobody can prove them, and that's the crux of the whole scene. Now, you get your ass out of here and leave us alone, or I'll charge you with harassment and see how you like a one- to five-year term on the rockpile!"

The followers all jumped up cheering and crowded behind Rivers, to show their support. Mark noticed that Tabler was among them. They all were shouting obscenities at him, questioning his parentage, and urging him to have intercourse with himself and all sorts of different animals. He didn't reply, just walked out the door. The last barb came from Tabler, who followed him to the porch.

"You slob. I bet your mother wears army boots," she said. Then, when she was sure none of the others could see her, she winked.

Joanna turned and went back inside the house and listened to the comments of the other members.

They were congratulating themselves on having put down the big Justice Department man.

"Really, you don't have to worry about that one or anything he said," Rivers reassured them. "He's a front man, a bluff. I've seen it a dozen times before. They threaten you with a felony, and you're supposed to weep and whimper and plead for mercy. Shit, they have to prove it all in court first. And proving just what they said we did last night would take a miracle. No way they could prove we set any of those fires or destroyed any government property or set off any bombs.

"Sure they can prove that someone did those things, but tying it down to a specific individual would be next to impossible unless they had a videotape or a series of photographs that positively identified a particular individual.

"So forget that guy. We have to concentrate on our next action. That's going to be an eight-hour picket line in front of the Labs parking lot. This will be a good one. Phil, you and Laurie get busy making the picket signs. Be sure the signs are all according to local laws and state laws. Some places the sticks that hold the signs can't be more than half an inch across."

She watched her team. "You're a good group. Now split for a while and let me do some thinking. Clutch and Melissa, you stay here."

The three of them sat in front of the small blaze in the fireplace, talking quietly.

"Last night was good for our group," Rivers said. "We had some real action, and we got busted. It has everyone worked up." Rivers narrowed her eyes thinking about it. "But what's next? How can we top that without really getting into trouble? I'm not going to put in any hard time for what I'm making on this deal."

Tabler tried not to react. Making on this deal? That sounded as if somebody had hired her to come here, giving her cash to perform the ritual here at the Labs at this particular time. Joanna saw Clutch turn and look at Rivers. Then Joanna charged into the quiet spot.

"How about a rally of some kind downtown? Marching through the business section with signs and banners. We jump on the atomic research they do at the Labs. We grind on the radiation scare, the genetic dangers—the pregnant women and preschoolers should all be prohibited from living in Los Alamos. That sort of emotional challenge. Radiation is very big now after the accidents."

Rivers nodded. "Melis, I think you have a good handle. Let Clutch and me talk it over. You better get the food ready. We've been eating a lot better since you joined us."

Tabler got up at once and went to the kitchen. Cooking was not her favorite work. Especially cooking for 20 people. But she was on the inside and getting evidence against Rivers. She didn't have enough to bring charges against Rivers yet, but it would come. She had to get enough to go into Federal court and come out with a conviction. Then Dan Griggs would be happy.

It had been fun seeing Mark today, even if it had been a bit of a confrontation. Mark really told them off. And she enjoyed yelling at him, then putting on the final wink to let him know she was only playing her part.

When was she going to get to see him again, alone? He was so near, yet so far. Tabler swore silently, inventing new combinations as she made lunch. It put her in exactly the right frame of mind.

Chapter 10

THE OLD DEADLY BADGER GAME

Mark left the Rivers school of ecology and drove to the center of the little town. He parked in front of the Smoketree Restaurant, where he hoped to find a platter-sized steak dripping with red juices. A gathering half way down the block attracted his attention and, curious, Mark walked in that direction. A newspaper rack got in his way. The headline caught his eye.

MURDER VICTIM FOUND HERE. The story gave the briefest of highlights. Sheriff Logan reported that a body with three bullet wounds in the chest had been found west of town at about one o'clock A.M. that day by a hitchhiker along a lonely stretch of Pelham Road. The victim was identified by papers on his body as being Matt Blumbert, 34, a white male whose last known address was in San Francisco. Tire tracks at the scene were not productive, and the police had no leads.

Additional details were promised in the next issue, including a driver's license picture of the man. Anyone with information about the dead man or his acquaintances was asked to contact the sheriff's department at once.

Mark walked on down to the gathering and found the high school band in full uniform, a speaker's stand, and one rack of bleachers. About a hundred people stood around watching. Mark listened for a minute to find out what it was all about.

"And I want to say, as mayor of Los Alamos, that all of us who live and work in this town, and at the Laboratories, have a profound and firm faith in the safety and well-being of our town and our families. We have no fears whatsoever about danger or trouble coming from the Labs. We are behind this government installation one thousand percent, and that's why we put together this little affirmative demonstration today, just to let our good friend and neighbor, Dr. Bill Dessel, know that we're pulling for him and that we know he and his crew out there are doing vital and important work for this great nation of ours.

"Now, let me introduce the chairman of our Chamber of Commerce business and industry committee, Mr. Harry Ackors, who will present the award of merit and approval to Dr. Dessel."

Mark watched a short, heavy man walk to the microphone, take the unit off the stand, and turn to the audience. His bald head gleamed in the morning sunshine. He grinned at the people.

"Most of you know I've been a good friend of Dr. Dessel for six or seven years now, ever since he came to town. I've watched him solve some of the darndest problems out at that think plant of his, and I can't know of anybody happier than I am to make this presentation today to Dr. Bill.

"The Labs mean more to this community than many of us realize. Sure, it's a big chunk of our economy—we know that and appreciate it. But too often we forget the other important aspects. Think of the uplifting influence of the well-educated men and women in our community. Think how they work in our various civic and cultural organizations and groups. Think how they help our churches and schools. I could go on and on, but I know that Dr. Dessel is anxious to get back to his work.

"Dr. Bill, let me say it again. This community is behind you one thousand percent. We'll do everything we can to help you in every way we can, and to further the glorious work you're doing out there. That's why it gives me a great deal of personal pleasure to present you with this, the Los Alamos Chamber of Commerce's Distinguished Citizen-of-the-Year award."

Mark watched Dr. Dessel take the plaque, say four or five muffled words of thanks out of range of the mike, wave to the applause of the audience, then hurry away.

The mayor took over the mike again and held up his hands for quiet.

"Ladies and gentlemen, I have a visitor to Los Alamos, and he said he came here for two reasons: to look over our local building situation and what we're putting up here, and to see the world-famous Los Alamos Laboratories here. He hoped that there was some kind of a tour he could take. Let me get him and his niece up here to talk for a minute. Here they are. This is Nicole and John Frank. They are from San Diego, where he's publisher of the *North County Contractor* magazine, as well as being a builder. Let's have a big round of applause for our visitors."

The audience gave them some weak clapping.

"John, I understand you just put up some condominiums in Hawaii—on Maui, if I'm correct."

"Yes, they're just finished."

"Good. John, I found out you're 33 years old, not

married, and you drive a flashy 280 SL Mercedes on this trip, a sparkling white one."

"Yes, right."

"And Nicole, who is about thirteen, is your niece. Nicole, you have beautiful light brown hair down to your shoulders. Do you have any hobbies?"

"I play tennis and I like to swim."

"Hey, that's fine, we have some of both here. Did you get a chance to tour the Laboratories?"

"We saw a little of them, but most of it is restricted," John said. "But we enjoyed what we saw."

"Good, good. Now, to help make your welcome here in Los Alamos complete and to encourage you to come back, we have some gifts and prizes for you. First is a week's free stay at the luxurious Freeway Motel, right here in town. Then you have a free pass for all the golf you can play at the Rolling Hills Country Club, and a weekend of free attendance at the Valley Tennis Club's famous tennis clinic.

"For the evenings we have a different delicious dinner for you and Nicole at six of our finest restaurants, and to please Nicole, we have for her a six-piece fun and play wardrobe from the Smarty Pants women's wear shop. How does all that sound?"

"Fine, wow! That's great," Nicole said.

"Well, we think it's fine too, Nicole and John, and we hope you tell your friends and neighbors back in San Diego that Los Alamos is a great place to visit. We want a whole lot of you to come see us. Let's have another big round of applause for our tourists of the week, John and Nicole Frank."

Mark worked his way through the crowd back to the restaurant, that big steak still on his mind.

The high school band played one last number as it marched away, and the crowd faded back into the stores, shops, and to the cars. Harry Ackors left the ceremony and walked straight to the Mountain State Savings and Loan. He nodded to several customers, went on through the small wooden gate, and into his private office. For once Mertha did not have any phone messages for him. He looked at a small notebook in his pocket and then asked Mertha to bring in the current list of delinquent loan accounts. There were about 25. He thanked her and she went back to her desk.

It took Ackors only ten minutes to pick out the man he wanted. His name was Willy Lockhart. He was three months behind on his mobile home payments, he just lost his job in the filling station, and his wife was working as a waitress to help them stay alive and feed the three kids. Willy also had spent three years with free room and board at the state pen for a small case of armed robbery.

Ackors dialed on his private phone line, which did not go through the company switchboard, and a moment later he was talking to Dawna Lane.

"I have a small job for you," Ackors said.

"Don't you always. What?"

"I'll give you a man's phone number. You are to offer him two hundred dollars to do a small bit of reverse mechanical work on two large diesel tractors at the Labs. He can get in and out through a hole in the fence about a mile past the gate. He probably knows the spot.

"He's to go to Building 176 and disable the two diesel tractors there. I don't care how he does it, but I don't want them running for at least a week. He'll get paid after the job. That's two hundred dollars. Got it?"

"Yes, Ackors, I've got it. No I don't need to write

it down. Yes, it was Building 176, and yes, I'll pay him after the dirty work is done."

"Christ, Miss Lane, you seem to be in a state today."

"In a state? Hell no, I'm furious. I always get the shit details, and you have all the fun. Now I have to move out of the house or go on paying the goddamn rent."

"Truly a fit of pique."

"What's the name and number?"

Ackors told her.

"Oh, great. This is the son of a bitch who tries to mount me every time he sees me in the grocery store."

"He has good taste."

"Sure, and bad breath and the clap and probably two or three other dandy diseases. I'll talk to him on the phone and then mail him the money."

"However you want to handle it. Just make damn sure that the work gets done."

"It will, fat man. It will. I know how to do my job."

"Then do it!" He slammed down the phone, angry at the bitch. She was probably in heat again. He had been good to her. She had all the money she wanted, she had the best assignments, and still she talked to him like he was dirt!

He trembled from his sudden outburst of temper. He had to maintain control at all times. Ackors took a dozen deep breaths, then picked up the phone and buzzed Mertha. "Do I have any appointments this afternoon?"

"Only one, Mr. Ackors, with the chamber committee."

"Call and tell them I can't make it. I'll be out for the rest of the day. Take any messages."

"Yes, Mr. Ackors."

He hung up, pushed the delinquent file to one corner of his desk, and went out the back door to his car.

The Skylark started as he gunned the motor loudly. Everyone told him that was hard on a car to make it roar that way before it was warmed up, but he couldn't break the habit, especially when he was mad. He drove straight to Dawna Lane's house and stopped half a block down the street. When he left his car, he had on a hat, heavily tinted sunglasses, and a different jacket. He went to the side door, opened it, and walked in.

Dawna was on the phone. She looked up, saw him, and frowned, then recognized Ackors and went back to the conversation.

"Yes, Willy. I'm intensely interested in seeing that the work is done and done right. I don't care how you do it." She listened. "That's right. Two hundred in cash when you're done and we hear our report back." She said something else quietly and hung up.

"You didn't have to spy on me. I know how to do a simple job like this one."

Ackors dropped the newspaper on her lap. "Of course you do. Just like you took out that nosey Justice Department man. You always get your man. Only this time you killed the wrong one. You eliminated the only reliable gunman I had in town."

"That Justice Department slob was out cold. I swear. I jammed a pin into him half an inch. Nobody can fake out that kind of surprise and pain."

"He must have. Or your juice wasn't good. He'll be back looking for you, and you better be ready.

Until he makes a move, we leave him alone, you understand? He looks like trouble all the way."

"Okay, you don't need to underline it in red. I have the picture."

"Still on a wild toot, aren't you? Okay, come into the bedroom, you need a lesson in technique."

"Oh, shit!"

"And a lesson in manners."

Dawna gritted her teeth, holding back what she really wanted to say. "Yes sir," was all she could manage before she marched ahead of him into the bedroom. She automatically began taking off her clothes, but he stopped her. Slowly he undid the buttons on the blouse, peeled it back, then unhooked her bra and let it fall off her ample breasts. He rubbed his face into her breasts and sucked on one, then he pulled her down beside him on the bed and took out a hand-rolled, brown-paper cigarette and lit it. She watched him with small, hard eyes as he pulled the smoke deep into his lungs and held it. He did the same thing three times, then he looked at her.

"Please, oh, please, just one or two tokes. I need it. Really!"

He laughed and suddenly the world seemed friendlier, brighter. He let the marijuana flood through his veins, let it mellow him and smooth away his anger. As she smoked, he stripped off her black pants and the blue nylon briefs under them. Then Ackors kissed her light brown thatch of crotch hair and laid her out on the bed.

Ackors took her savagely the first time, not worrying if she were ready or pleased or happy. She let the pot sway her, and soon she was feeling as sexy as he was, and together they wove a fantastic spell of wild and strange positions and unusual combinations.

At last they collapsed on the bed and came out of the happy land about four that afternoon. First they ate, then he stared at her in the light blue housecoat. He told her to stand up and open the garment. Ackors poked at her thighs and waist.

"Lose ten pounds," he said. "You're my key playing card. You have to stay fit and trim and sexy."

"That's easy for you to say, chubby."

"You can't get me upset now, not again. Because tonight you will put on the best performance of your life. Tonight you will seduce Dr. William Dessel."

Her eyes widened in astonishment. "Dr. Dessel, the director? Old stick in the mud? How in the world am I going to screw him? He's stuffy, he's cold, and he's married."

Ackors scratched his naked belly and laughed. "That, my little cactus flower, is why it will be so much simpler than you might even suspect."

At seven that evening, Dr. Dessel rang the bell at Dawna's front door. She had dressed carefully, a tight white blouse buttoned to the neck, a moderately tight skirt of blue velvet, and high heels. Her short brown hair was brushed until it glowed in soft splendor, and she had spent half an hour on her make-up to be sure she was as striking as possible.

Dr. Dessel came in and hardly noticed her.

"Well, what have you to tell me that's so important?" he said, one notch above brusqueness.

"Dr. Dessel, this is going to be very hard for me, do you mind if we sit down?"

He frowned, walked to the first chair, a big overstuffed one, and sat stiffly. It was obvious he did not like Dawna and was there only because she might have some vital information for him.

She sat on the couch opposite him.

"You said you had something tell me about Stanley, someone he had been talking to, someone pressuring him, you thought, to get scientific data from him about the LONG REACH program."

"Yes, I think so. I can't be sure. I said I'd tell you exactly what happened. I think I can remember." She stopped and slowly, gradually, she broke up and began crying. He looked at her, surprised and bewildered.

"Miss Lane. I didn't know that you were so worried, so upset . . . I mean, I'm sorry if I have been too abrupt."

She tried to calm down, drying the real tears, stopping the sobs. It was a slow process.

"This is so . . . I didn't think I would break up that way. Dr. Dessel, I'm sorry. I would like some tea to help steady my nerves. Would you care for some with me?"

"No."

"Please, I would feel so much better if you had some too. It'll only take a few seconds."

He nodded.

She made the tea in the kitchen and put five drops from a small brown bottle into his cup, stirred it in well, and disguised it with a slice of lemon.

Back in the living room, she offered him cream and sugar. He took both.

She sipped her tea and began. "I guess the first time I noticed it was when he got a phone call, and he asked me to turn down the TV sound or close the door. I closed the door. The next time . . . Dr. Dessel. Is there something wrong with your tea?"

"Oh, no, it's fine." He took a long swallow, then another. She had made the tea only slightly warm on purpose. "Something made you suspicious about the phone call?"

"Well, not at first, but then he kept getting more calls." She stopped and drank from her tea. "Can I get more tea for you?"

"This is fine." He took another few swallows and the cup was down to half.

"I answered the phone once, and a man with an accent of some kind asked for Stanley. He suggested I leave the room while he talked shop with the man. I knew there wasn't anyone with an accent like that on the project. And I couldn't even remember a foreigner who talked that way in the Labs."

"What kind of an accent was it?" Dr. Dessel asked, and blinked. Then he frowned and rubbed his eyes.

"I don't remember now, German, maybe. I'm not very good on languages."

Dr. Dessel shook his head. He lifted the tea cup and drained it, then put it down with a clatter.

"I'm sorry. I felt sleepy there for a moment. The tea will help me." He rubbed his head. "Everything is fine now."

"Why don't you just lean back there for a moment, then you'll feel better."

"I . . . Oh, my Lord, but I'm getting fuzzy. I don't know what is happening." He blinked again, then struggled to hold his eyes open. "I think I better get home."

"You can't drive feeling this way."

He tried to stand, staggered to his feet, then his eyes closed, he sagged, and she pushed him onto the sofa, where he gave her one pained, baleful look, and passed out.

Dawna waited a few moments, then stuck him with the pin, and she knew he was unconscious. She tapped on the bedroom door, and Harry Ackors came from the room. He had taken a nap and was refreshed and ready for action. Quickly he checked Dr. Dessel, then drove the director's car close to the side door. It was fully dark now as he and Dawna struggled out the door with the scientist and put him in the back seat. He was half on the floor but he wouldn't notice the discomfort.

The drug they used was a new one, and Ackors's superiors said it would knock out a man in a few minutes and leave him fuzzy-minded and hazy as to where he had been or what he had done for 16 to 18 hours before he took it. A kind of short-lived amnesia. Ackors hoped it worked that way.

They drove to a motel on the far side of town, the Sleepy Inn. It was an older, run-down establishment, now used partly by weekly and monthly low-income renters. Tourists passed it by unless it had the last room available.

They parked to shield the motel door with the car and got Dr. Dessel into the motel room. He was still unconscious, and it would be about a half-hour more before the drug wore off.

Inside they lay him on the bed and stripped him, folding his clothes precisely and putting them over a chair the way they guessed the scientist might do it.

Ackors was surprised how young the girl was when she came to the door. He figured she was about 19, hard looking, a dirty blonde, with long hair and eyes that were cold and cynical, yet ready and willing to do almost anything for a few dollars. She glanced at the naked man.

"God, he's hung. Is he the one or are you?"

Ackors laughed. "Look, young whore. I don't have to pay for my pussy. Now get your clothes off and let's take a look at your goodies." He waved Dawna out the door. She would wait in her car across the street until he called her.

The young girl looked at him, then at Dr. Dessel, and her eyes twitched, then she fumbled with her purse. "I don't think I want this trick. Here's the fifty bucks back she gave me. It looks too kinky even for me."

Ackors slapped her across the face, shoving her against the bed. She almost fell. He grabbed her and slammed her head against the wall once, then his hand slid up to her throat, and he choked her until she sagged. Ackors was breathing heavily now, and he felt his erection. God, but this was going to be good! He checked to be sure she was still breathing, the girl had to be alive. She was and he dropped her on the bed and began stripping off her clothes.

A little over a half-hour later, Dr. William Dessel, director of the Los Alamos Experimental Laboratories and newly designated Los Alamos Citizen-of-the-Year, blinked and stared half-seeing at the ceiling. His face worked, and one hand came up and rubbed his face, and he looked upward again. He tried to sit, but the pounding in his head pushed him down. The first flare of alarm touched him. This was a strange room, and he was in a bed—a motel room, he decided. How in the world did he get in a motel room? He was on a bed, under a sheet. My God! He was naked! There were his clothes, as he had folded them. Slowly he turned and looked beside him.

"Oh, Lord!" he said softly. There was another form under the sheets beside him. Had he taken some floozy to a motel? Who? Why? He sat up and his motion pulled the sheet away from the head of the person who was lying there. A young woman with long blonde hair. He couldn't see her face. Dr. Dessel sat there a moment. He would slip out while she slept. Yes! But when he tried to move again, his head pounded and he almost fell on top of her. He got out of bed at last with a great deal of effort. When he walked around the foot of the bed for his clothes, he saw that part of the sheet over her was stained.

For just a moment he rejected the idea. But it was fact. He was a scientist, he dealt only with facts. The stain was red. Oh, Jesus, no! His first impulse was that she was sick or hurt, or perhaps she had injured herself after . . . after . . . God, what would he tell Martha? His wife was understanding, mature, and reasonable, but this! . . .

He couldn't make himself touch the sheet. It draped over a white shoulder, showed part of one breast and the edge of her face. Then he bit into his lower lip until he tasted his own blood. He had to look! He had to be sure she was all right before he left, no matter who she was. With a sudden movement he grabbed the edge of the sheet and threw it back.

Dr. William Dessel gave a low cry and knew he was going to pass out. The bed reeled at him, the mass of cuts and blood swarmed up at him, and he fell, sprawling across her bloody legs on the foot of the bed.

Harry Ackors had watched the little drama. Now he opened the bathroom door all the way and stepped out. He understood why Dr. Bill Dessel had been shocked into unconsciousness. The girl lay on her back—one breast had been cut off her chest and lay beside her. Her stomach had been deeply slashed with crisscrossing marks, and all had bled profusely. Her right hand had been amputated at the wrist and lay on her throat. Both legs were sliced with deep gouges, and one eyeball hung obscenely on her cheek. From all appearances, the girl had bled to death. She had been alive when she was slashed, so there had been a maximum amount of pain and blood.

Harry Ackors smiled. Yes, no wonder the perceptive Dr. Dessel passed out. Ackors went up to the director and began slapping him gently on his face.

"Bill, wake up! Bill for God's sake, wake up!"

It took several moments to get Bill Dessel back to consciousness. As he worked on the man, Ackors checked his precautions. The motel was the sex connection for half of Los Alamos. Here was where most of the quickie sexsploits took place. The management was used to it—in fact, encouraged it with rooms rented by the two-hour time period. Dawna had made the reservations and picked up the key. She had signed in as Mr. and Mrs. Brown. She told them it was a fraternity thing, a pair of boys from Santa Fe, and she would pay for any damages. He relaxed. All of the obvious problems were covered.

"Bill, wake up! Come on, dammit, wake up!"

Dr. Dessel groaned, then he tried to roll over and recoiled in horror. He jumped off the bed and out of contact with the girl. Blood stained both his hands, and now his legs.

He saw Harry. "Jesus, Harry. Jesus!" He began to cry great, wracking sobs.

Ackors pulled him away from the bed.

"Bill, snap out of it. We don't have time for that, not yet!"

Dr. Dessel choked off his sobbing and slashed at the tears. He wouldn't look at Ackors. "Jesus, Harry, what the hell happened? What are you doing here?"

"Trying to help you, if you'll let me."

"I don't know anything about this. Honest to God I don't!"

He turned to look at Harry now, but saw the girl instead with the bloody, tortured body. He ran to the bathroom and vomited in the tub. When his stomach was empty, he washed out his mouth.

"Harry, what is this? I've never seen that girl before."

"Bill, all I know is I had a phone call from the manager here who said you were in trouble, and he saw me introduce you this noon at the presentation, so he called me. He said you were in some bad trouble and I should get down here right away. I had no idea . . . I mean, Bill. . . ."

"So help me God, Harry. I don't know her. I didn't bring her here. I don't remember her or any presentation ceremony or today. I don't even remember going to work this morning. Presentation ceremony? What presentation?"

Harry Ackors stared at his friend for several seconds. Then he shrugged.

"Okay, Bill. I'm not here to judge you or throw stones. You don't have to do a thing. I got a little rough with a whore one time myself. I'm not putting you down. We all get carried away. You were probably on something, pills she gave you, maybe she put something in your drink. The combination can be wild."

"Harry. I never touch that poison. I wouldn't know how to contact a whore. Even if I did . . . I never would hurt . . . I mean somebody tortured this poor girl. A body doesn't bleed like that after it's dead. So that means she was cut up that way before. . . ."

"Bill, forget that. Now you get your damn clothes on so we can get you out of here. Can you do that?"

Dr. Dessel nodded.

"Good, get dressed fast, and I'll see what we should do. There is no way we call Bill Logan on this. He'd have you in jail for a year before he figured out what to do."

Dr. Dessel had just slid into his underwear and pants. He looked up. "We've got to call Logan. I'm in enough trouble now."

"Bill, you're not thinking straight yet. It must be the pills. You call in the sheriff now and you're in jail, period. You are on trial without a doubt. And there might have been five or six people who saw you come in here if they try to remember. The manager called me, so he knows you're here, and he knows that I know you're here. We'd both have to testify against you. You wouldn't have a chance of a snowcone in an oven of beating this. We can't call in the sheriff."

Bill Dessel looked across the room. He glanced away from her body quickly. "But she was a real person. She was alive. If I killed her . . . if I did, then . . . God, then I should be put away!"

"Bill, no. You're a special person. What if you made a little mistake here? She was a whore anyway. She's a nothing. You're too valuable to our town, to the country. Think about that. Now, no more arguments. Get into your clothes quickly. We can never tell how much time we have left. She might have screamed. Logan might be on the way here right now."

Dr. Dessel finished dressing, still not able to look at the carved-up girl on the bed. He shivered as he tried to get his shoes tied. Then they went to the door.

Harry touched his shoulder. "Bill, we've been good friends for years. I've never known you to do anything illegal or out of line, let alone something crazy and horrible like this. I'd bet my whole company that you didn't do this. You've got to believe that, or you'll drive yourself nuts. Now say it. Say that you did not kill this girl, that you didn't have anything to do with it."

Dr. Dessel said it once, then again.

Ackors poked him on the shoulder. "Right, now I'll get this cleaned up. I don't know how, yet, but I'll take care of it. That's what friends are for. You don't think about it again. Just keep in mind that you didn't do it and that you're going to go on with your work and your life as usual. Make absolutely sure that you go to work in the morning. Got that?"

He sighed. "I'll try, Harry. I don't know how I'm ever going to be able to . . ."

"Bill, that's what real friends are for. Now let me look outside."

Ackors stepped out the door. Dr. Dessel glanced at the bed and shuddered as he looked away. He moved to the door, touched his pockets to make sure he had all of his things, then edged the door open.

Ackors had driven a car near the room and was getting out.

"My God, Harry, that's my car," Bill Dessel said softly.

"I saw it out there and it had the keys in it. It looked like the only way. Some of the best license plates in the county drive in here from time to time. Bill, get in and go home and take it easy. Drive carefully. Let me worry about the rest of this. And go to work tomorrow."

"I should help you. It's my problem."

"Now, it's our problem, Bill. So you get the hell out of here."

He slid into the car and looked out the window.

"Harry, if there's anything I can do for you . . . I mean anything, you let me know. You just saved my life."

"Don't worry about it, Bill. Now get moving, I've got some work to do."

Dr. William Dessel closed the car window, pulled a cap down over his eyes, and drove slowly out of the motel lot and into the street.

Harry Ackors spent the next hour cleaning up the motel room. He put the dead girl in a heavy plastic body bag he had brought and pushed it into the trunk of his own car. Then he called Dawna. She went to the office, roused the night clerk, and told him she owed him some extra money. They looked at the room, saw the blood, and she told him not to worry. It was only a fraternity initiation, and it was all chicken blood, nobody even got scratched, but one kid got the shit scared out of him. The night clerk chuckled, remembering a similar incident years ago in which he took part.

He scratched his crotch. "Hell, I'd say a new

mattress and the bedding, and cleaning. It'll all come to a hundred and forty dollars."

"No way, that's robbery. I'll replace them myself and do it for less than a hundred. I'll give you seventy-five bucks."

He reached out and deliberately rubbed one of her breasts. She didn't move or react.

"You've got damn good tits. I'll make you a deal. An even hundred bucks and one long slow, the rest of the night fucking party in my bed."

She watched him a minute. He would expect it, it would help cover up the whole thing. "Hell yes, why not? I'm saving forty bucks. It's a deal."

From across the street in his car, Ackors watched Dawna come out of the death room with the manager and go into the office with the man. Five minutes later she hadn't come out, and the exterior light snapped off. Harry Ackors swore. Now he'd have to dig the damn hole all by himself. He shrugged and drove away. It was better this way, cleaner. If she ever got unhappy, she wouldn't know where the body was buried. That made him feel a lot better.

Ackors grinned as he remembered the shock on the whore's face when she came to after he had choked her. He was humping her like crazy, and she hadn't even known it. That was a trip in itself!

Harry hummed as he drove into the back country. He knew exactly the right place for a grave that would never be found.

Chapter 11

WRONG-HANDED DEATH RAY

The next morning, Mark was outside Dr. Dessel's office when he came to work at eight o'clock A.M. The scientist looked tired and worn, and only nodded at Mark as they went into the office. It took Mark five minutes to get a word from the man. He simply stood at his window and looked out at a small gardenlike alcove.

"Dr. Dessel, I know this is hard for you, but you simply have to face up to it all. The guards told me that two of the tractors have been sabotaged, but that they have replacements for them. Put it all together, and it's a strong hand playing against you. The girl is a suspect in the death of two of your top scientists. The explosion with the pick-up, the environmentalists showing up at just this time. And add to that, someone tried to kill me. It's a lot of trouble." Mark watched him. Dr. Dessel seemed to have trouble concentrating.

"Yes, Mr. Zilke. I know. I'm . . . we're trying to do something about all of this right now."

"What are you doing?"

"What? Oh, guards. We've doubled them, put them on full alert now."

"Is that all?" Mark asked.

"What else can I do? I can't call out the National Guard or order up a division of Marines. I'm working it out the best way I can. After all, I do have a budget I must stay within."

"With your kind of connections and clout, you could get all the help you need. Yell to Washington. Ask them to send in a battalion of GIs on some kind of field training exercise. Get a company of Marines on loan. Do something. Talk to your boss in Washington. You've got heavy influence back there."

"What? Oh, yes, Zilke. I'll have to do that. Now I have a conference coming up."

"It's not a conference, it's a test shot. I'm going to be there, Dr. Dessel, so you might as well give me a test badge."

Dr. William Dessel seemed to sag a little. Then he opened his desk and handed Mark three clip-on badges.

"The other two are for your FBI friends," he said and stood.

Mark took the hint and left the office. He wondered about the director. He seemed vague, fuzzy, tired, and not concentrating this morning. Maybe he was just worried about the shot coming up.

At the office, Mark gave the FBI men the test badges and Sanchez yelped in delight.

"Hey, damn! I'm glad you got these. I was going if I had to sneak in."

Goodman flipped his on the desk. He was working on a thick file and had two more on the desk. "Sorry, Zilke, I won't have time. I'm working on a new line of reasoning on this damn Penetrator. The bastard is a Mexican—a Chicano—a Mexican-American, whatever you want to call him, and I think he's probably a half-breed. Maybe half Mex, maybe only a quarter. That's why he looks like he has a good sun tan all the time. Now, if I work backward from that and try to dig into that first Los Angeles hit he made, I think I can score and get a positive I.D. on the son of a bitch. Once I have that, I'm halfway home to nailing the bastard."

"Lots of luck, Goodman, but what about our problem right here?" Mark asked.

Goodman glanced up in disgust. "Damn, you really think there's a legitimate case here? Nothing but a weird batch of scientists getting themselves killed over some Buck Rogers kind of ray gun that will never work. I've got more important things to do."

"You still want to sign the reports to D.C. that I'm making up every day on this case?" Sanchez asked.

"Oh, hell yes. I don't want to upset the boys at the Bureau." Goodman chuckled to himself and went back to his Penetrator file.

Sanchez's eyes darkened, and his face tightened with anger. He grabbed the badge Mark had given him, picked up his jacket, and left the room. Mark followed.

"When that slob has something to add to one of my reports or gives me some input, then he can sign it. Not until," Sanchez told Mark. He let some of his frustration boil out through his face, then he sighed. "Hell, let's get out to the shoot. Why did they send him in here senior to me?"

The Labs bus dropped them off at the same area where Mark had been before. The heavy trucks were all lined up, and the betatron gun trailer was parked at the brink of the hill. Evidently there were replacement trucks for the ones damaged. As Mark looked around, there didn't seem to be as many technicians this time, and at least five or six fewer trucks. Mark counted about 20 techs. Dr. Dessel walked by, and Mark asked him about it.

"We're starting to streamline our firing procedures, to get them down so two or three men can do it. Eventually it all will be done by one man at a ground panel through radio control." He moved on toward the command trailer, his hands deep in his white lab coat pockets.

Preparations continued for the shot. Then the public address system cut in and Mark listened.

"This is Target One. We have a problem. A woman is here and says her name is H. R. Rivers. She tells us there is no way we can make our shot today. She has taken over Target One by force of arms and has four other women sitting around the target. Check your scopes, please, or the monitor."

At almost the same time the loudspeakers quieted, there was a staccato roar of automatic weapons fire from both sides of the line of trucks. Two men ran into the area from each side, waving rapid-fire submachine guns. One took over the command trailer and its communications. There were no armed guards on the site.

"Attention on the shot site," the P.A. blared. It was a man's voice. "This is the voice of the people speaking. There will be no experimental shot here this afternoon unless we the people authorize it. We have complete control of your position. Our weapons are fully automatic, but we don't want to kill any of you unless we have to. The four men now among you with the MP-40 submachine guns are all combat veterans who know how to fight and have killed before. So don't tempt us. Simply follow your orders quickly and precisely from this trailer and all will be fine."

Now Mark saw a dozen more of the Western Naturalists filter into the position. All had handguns or the German made MP-40s. Mark was familiar with the weapon. It was used by many terrorists and could fire 9mm cartridges at the rate of 500 rounds a minute. The muzzle velocity was something like 1200 to 1300 feet per second. A nasty little weapon.

Mark felt stymied. They had the control center, the command post. He could take out a few of them, but were they sheep or goats, innocents or actually candidates for death?

He and Sanchez dodged behind a truck.

"What the hell can we do now?" Sanchez asked.

"You have your piece?"

"Sure, a .38 with a two-inch barrel, but it won't go up against a damned MP-40."

"Depends how close you are. You work around one side. See if you can surprise one of those guys with the chatter gun. If we can eliminate two or three of those quietly, we'll have a better chance. But we don't want a fire fight in here with all these civilians."

"Right. Surprise them. I'm with you. I'll go to this side."

He moved away from the control truck. Mark worked toward it. He passed two girls with handguns who didn't seem to know what to do with them. One of the girls giggled. The others would fade away if he got Rivers. She was the key, but where was she? This was the logical spot for her to show. He kept watching. Then a Jeep pulled up and Rivers jumped out of it. She had an MP-40, an

ERMA, in one hand and ran into the command trailer.

The P.A. came on at once.

"This is Rivers speaking. I'm with the WNU, the Western Naturalists United. We're going to close down this whole damn program. But before we do, let's let the little white-coated men set up their next shot. Our people have evacuated the number-one target area to the safe zone as stipulated by your guards at the site. So you are now free to go ahead and aim and generate or whatever the hell you do to complete the shot."

Mark had moved to within 50 feet of the command trailer when he heard the speakers come on again. He was not showing his weapon, but the trusty .45 was in his shoulder leather. He hadn't brought Ava along. He didn't think he would need it.

One of the MP-40s went off near him, and Mark looked up to see a large black man holding the weapon aimed at the sky. The man laughed and let go with another burst. The man was Clutch Washington, who had come out of college and gone right into the NBA. He'd never been in 'Nam.

Mark couldn't move. Washington was watching him now. The countdown and preparations for the shot continued. Then five minutes after Rivers had given the go-ahead, the final command came through.

"Fire, Fire, Fire!"

Mark had no idea what the target was. They had not brought along the video screens this time.

The loudspeakers snapped on. "How did you do this shot? Did you kill that poor cow ten miles from here?" The voice was Rivers'. There was a pause.

"This magnificent specimen of human kindness has just confirmed, ladies and gentlemen, that his weapon has roasted alive an innocent Hereford cow at the ten-mile range. Isn't that just a marvel of science?" Her voice dripped with disdain.

"Now, forget about the second test. My people are there and have been instructed to stay. They are armed and ready to fight to remain in that position. You see that building down here about a mile? Let's see what your ray gun can do to that." There was loud talk, some yelling, and then a single sharp report of a gun going off. It all came over the loudspeakers.

"Don't panic, anyone, or do anything foolish. That was a shot, true. And it went through the roof of this aluminum tin can. The next three go through Dr. Dessel's forehead unless he gets things in gear and fires at that building. Do I make myself clear? Now aim the damn ray gun where I told you."

There was another silence. It stretched out. Clutch Washington had moved away, and Mark edged toward the trailer. A small girl with a big .45 in her hand motioned at Mark to stop. She walked up to within 3 feet of him and pointed the .45 at his stomach.

"No farther. I've been watching you. Sit down," she said.

"Hell no," Mark said. "Your boss just came out of the control van, and she's waving at me to go over there."

The girl did not turn and look. "Bullshit."

Mark saw her finger begin to tighten on the trigger.

"I said sit down, big man."

Mark looked at the safety on the .45. It was still

in place. She could pull the trigger as hard as she wanted to and it wouldn't fire. Mark moved, not seemingly fast, but before the girl knew it, he had slapped the weapon from her hand and pushed her down behind the wheels of a truck. Mark tightened plastic riot cuffs around her ankles and wrists and used her own dirty kerchief to make a simple, no-danger gag. He left her under the wheels of the truck and moved again toward the trailer.

The loudspeaker voices jolted him.

"We are at speed."

"Yes, I have voltage. Proper voltage."

"Fire, Fire, Fire!"

Now Mark was near enough to the command van so he could see the small TV monitor set outside. A dozen technicians and a few ecology people watched. A small building showed on the screen, and just as the command to fire was given, a half-ton pick-up drove from behind the building to the front.

Mark saw it happen, saw the metal blister and puff with smoke as the paint burned off the truck, then the tremendous heat vaporized the gas in the tank and the vapor ignited with a visual explosion they couldn't hear. The small wooden building behind gushed into flames from the spewing, cascading, burning gasoline.

"Oh my God!" somebody said softly.

The rest watched without a word, too stunned to cry out. Nobody moved.

Then a figure jumped from the control van. It was H. R. Rivers. Mark ripped his eyes away from the monitor and made certain it was the ecology leader. She ran toward the betatron truck on the lip of the hill 20 yards away. Already people were disconnecting the huge umbilical electrical cords. By the time she got there, the truck was free. Mark started after her but saw three of the machinegun-toting guards around the big International diesel tractor. She swung up into the cab, and that was when Mark realized the diesel tractor's engine was running. The big rig was ready to move. The exhaust belched a cloud of black smoke, and the rig pulled away at a crawl. Its top speed was only 10 miles an hour. The driver evidently didn't know that.

Mark reversed his direction and ran at full speed behind the row of trucks to cut off the crawling betatron low-boy trailer-tractor rig. He had no idea what he would do when he got there. It was still his .45 against three or four submachine guns. As he got to the end of the line of trucks, he noticed that the last three in line had their motors idling. They must be the first trucks to leave at the conclusion of the test.

Mark leaped into one truck without a driver and touched the fuel pedal on the big Peterbilt tractor. Mark slammed it into first gear and let out on the clutch, jolting ahead, but he was moving. He shifted into second in high range and rolled another 20 feet as he overfuelled the laboring diesel, but he kept it moving ahead. Mark's Peterbilt with its 40-foot trailer came out at right angles to the slow-moving International pulling the betatron, and he could move ten times as fast.

That was when Mark saw Clutch Washington sitting astride the International's big hood. He held his submachine gun and aimed it directly at the Peterbilt. Mark held the wheel tightly on the collision course and dropped down sideways on the seat just before the window glass shattered as the 9mm slugs tore through the Pete's windows and windshield. At the end of the five-round burst, Mark jolted up, checked his direction, then dropped down before Washington triggered a new spurt of rounds. The second burst slammed into the Peterbilt's hood, dug through the metal, and pounded into the engine block, oil filter, and various nonvital engine components. But the burst couldn't stop the 425-horsepower giant. Mark dodged up to check his course again, spun the wheel to the right, and slammed head-on into the International at 10 miles an hour.

Clutch Washington's submachine gun had swung down with a clear shot at Mark in the cab, but the head-on collision ruined his aim. A stream of seven slugs crashed into the cab roof, and Mark lifted his Detonics .45 and punched two big holes in Clutch's chest right over his heart, cartwheeling the big man off the truck hood.

Two other gunmen with automatic weapons fell almost at the same time, one to Sanchez's marksmanship from up close, and the other when he was knocked down by an angry, surging group of a dozen technicians who didn't want to see their project ruined. He could have killed most of them with the submachine gun, but the young man had never shot at anyone before in his life and couldn't pull the trigger.

Mark saw Rivers leap from the other side of the International and grab Clutch's dropped MP-40 as she ran for the cover of the other trucks.

A snarling .38 cut up the dust in front of her, turning her back toward the cliff. Mark ran across an open space to another truck, saw he wouldn't make it before she fired, so dove and rolled the last 6 feet to safety. Her automatic fire chewed up the turf behind him in three-round bursts but missed.

"Throw it down, Rivers, you don't have a chance. You only have seventeen rounds left before your magazine runs dry. Then we push you right over the cliff." Mark made it sound as mean and angry as possible.

She put a three-round burst into the truck Mark hid behind, then ran the other way.

Mark heard Sanchez yell at her, say he was FBI, and that she couldn't get out that way. She stopped for a moment in frustration. Then she ran back toward Mark, firing as she came. Mark aimed under the truck, led her, and fired. He had aimed at her thighs, and he caught the left one, spun her around, and she fell sideways into the dirt. She dropped the submachine gun but grabbed it again.

"Don't lift it off the ground, lady, or you're stone dead," Mark yelled from his cover 20 feet away.

"Rivers, I'll help you!" It was Joanna Tabler. She shouted, then sprinted between two trucks. "He won't kill both of us!"

Before Rivers could react, Joanna rushed forward, her .38 waving in the air. Mark hoped that Sanchez didn't get excited and fire. He didn't.

Joanna reached Rivers but instead of falling in front of her for protection, Joanna kicked the MP-40 out of River's hands and dropped on top of her so the ecology leader couldn't move.

Mark ran up and put riot cuffs on Rivers, then cut open her jeans and looked at the wound. He ripped off half of his white shirt and made a bandage with it and a compress and tied up the wound tightly. Rivers didn't say a word.

Sanchez had led the job of rounding up the rest of the ecology nuts. All of them threw away their guns and tried to run, but the technicians collared them and sat them down in a small ring between the trucks. Clutch Washington, beside the International tractor, was dead. A truck went for the rioters at the number-two target, and they came peacefully when they were told what happened.

Another team checked the small building still burning below. Both men in the truck were dead. They had been picking up some routine outdoor tests and had nothing to do with the LONG REACH program.

Mark guessed that all of the ecology freaks would be charged with conspiracy, and some of them would face a murder rap, including Rivers.

"Is it over?" Tabler asked.

"Far from over. Rivers here is just a counterploy, one more try by the team. The head man is the one we need." Mark looked at Rivers. Her face was dirty, her T-shirt sagging, and he knew her leg pained her severely.

"Who hired you, Rivers? Who paid you to bring your circus to town this particular week to try to stop the tests?"

She didn't respond.

Joanna put her hand on the thigh wound and pushed down hard.

Rivers screamed, but still she didn't speak. She glared at Joanna, then passed out.

Mark reached over and kissed Joanna. "You always did have a gentle touch when it came to persuasion," he said.

Chapter 12

KILL TRY TIMES SIX

Harry Ackors paced up and down in his big house on Alder Street. From the information he had from the test shot today at the Labs, they had perfected the weapon, even though H. R. Rivers had waded in and bungled things grandly. Now it was only a matter of engineering it down into a composite field unit. That was simple work and wouldn't take long. He had failed at his basic assignment.

Ackors paced again. The work of the ecologists had served him for a time, and their fate didn't concern him. He had used them as he would anyone he could. The Rivers woman was a complete idiot to try what she did. She was lucky not to be dead by now.

His own shadow crossed the room in front of him, and it brought a sudden sweat to his brow. His shadow agent. He hadn't thought about his shadow for a long time. He had no idea who the person might be, but it must be someone there in town. If he failed in this mission or became captured or compromised, the shadow agent would move in and eliminate him in minutes. That way he would not be an embarrassment to the mother country. But he hadn't failed totally. He had slowed the project down over the past three years, and that had been his job. Now the program was nearly complete. He sat down and put his face in his hands.

What he needed was a bold move, a counterstroke they wouldn't anticipate! That might be enough to save him. It would have to be extreme, brilliant, effective. He began thinking. He would use Dawna—she was the only one he had trained to be reliable enough for something like this.

How to do it? Burn down the whole Labs complex? No. Hire a plane to bomb the Labs off the map? Good, but he had no ordinance that would do the job. He had to do something else. He thought through a dozen ideas before the one that made enough sense and was workable surfaced. He called Dawna and told her to come to his house at once and bring her list of Labs employees and their addresses.

It was just after dark when Dawna, dressed in men's clothes, rang the bell at Dr. Vincent Leslie's home. He lived alone and she knew he was home. He came to the door, snapped on the porch light, and grinned when he saw her.

"Hey, Dawna! What a great surprise. Come on in."

She went inside and he closed the door. "Hello, Vince. Got a minute and a shoulder to cry on?"

"Of course, for you, sweetheart, any time."

She smiled then thrust the 6-inch knife upward under his rib cage, rammed it in to the hilt, and then slashed sideways at his heart and aorta. At once she felt his arm slide off her shoulder. He fell to the hallway, blood gushing from the fatal wound. He would die within minutes. She stared down at him with a twinge of regret, then dropped the knife from her gloved hand and went out the front door after snapping off the porch light.

One down, two to go.

Dr. Martin Brokowski had not asked for protection, but Sheriff Logan insisted on it. Logan had spent three years as a cop in the Lower East Side of New York City, and he had an instinct for the criminal mind. He figured the next strike would be at the weakest link at the Labs, the scientists themselves. He had one man inside Brokowski's house and another one outside in an unmarked police car.

They should have nailed him. The man walked the last half-block so the outside man wasn't alerted. As it was, Deputy Clawson expected nothing. When a man went up to the Brokowski door, the deputy came alert but was not worried. The door opened, and the first shot brought Clawson out of his car, unholstering his 6-inch-barreled .357 magnum. The house door swung open again and a small, fat man was outlined in the light for a second, then disappeared. Deputy Clawson had one shot at the man as he dove through a new hedge into the next yard. Clawson started in pursuit but stumbled over a bicycle left in the yard and broke his ankle. By the time the inside deputy got to the yard, the attacker was on the next street, and they never did find him. The shot that the fat man had fired had missed both the lawman and Brokowski, who had started for the door.

Harry Ackors cursed his luck. There was no reason they should put guards on the scientists. It had been a lucky guess on their part. He panted from his three-block run. Much more of this, and he would take off the 30 pounds the doctor had told him to. It had been simple—knock on the door and hit Brokowski with a shot in the heart when he opened the door. Only it wasn't the scientist who answered the knock. It was a sheriff's deputy with his hand on his six-gun. At least the deputy forgot to turn on the light and Ackors was certain that the kid hadn't recognized him. The man was new to the force. Besides, Ackors had on his fake beard and floppy hat.

He put his car into gear and drove away slowly. Should he make another try? He would at least check out one more home. He'd try the only unmarried one on his list of three.

Dan Streib was older than most of the others, he had just turned 50 and was the second man from the top in the LONG REACH program. He was an expert in charged particles and had an extensive background in all kinds of accelerators. Streib was the key man in down-sizing the current betatron so they could put one in space.

He lived on the edge of town on a little ranch, with a few trees, five acres, and a ramshackle house that needed a lot of repairs, but the professor never found time to do the work.

Ackors parked down the road and walked through a field, coming up behind the house. It had two lights on. He peered through the first window, which was the living room, and found no one there. The next window was higher and opened into the kitchen.

Dr. Streib stood at the range, working on something in a skillet.

Ackors took a .45 from his belt. It would punch a slug through the window and the screen and not vary a millimeter in its presighted and deadly flight path.

Ackors held the heavy .45 with both hands and sighted down. He couldn't afford to make any more mistakes. Mr. Smith would never forgive him. Not now.

He sighted in again and just before his finger tightened on the trigger, somebody at the corner of the house yelled, then fired. Ackors felt his hand jerk to the side as his .45 went off, and at the same instant something smashed into him, burning, ripping, tearing into his left shoulder. He staggered back, fired instinctively at his enemy, and saw the two slugs rip into the deputy. Then Ackors turned and ran through the field. He didn't look back to see if anyone were following. He ran in a rage, fury and sorrow and frustration all piling one on top of another. How could they have known he would try for more than one of the men? Did they cover all of them?

At his car he drove quickly back toward his house, fearful of some kind of a radio-alerted roadblock. There was none. He turned off his route and went instead to Dawna's place. He saw a light on in the living room and continued past half a block. Ackors parked, then went through the vacant lot in back and in the left side door of Dawna's house. He made sure no one saw him slip inside.

Dawna lay face down on the sofa. She heard him come in.

"Harry?"

"Yes." He held his shoulder as blood dripped off his fingers into the red shag rug. "I've been hit."

A half-hour later, she had treated his shoulder wound, powdering it with penicillin, sterilizing it, and bandaging it tightly. The slug had taken a deep half-inch groove out of his upper shoulder, scraped the bone, and gone on its way.

"One down out of three for me," she said.

"Leslie. He was alone and not expecting company. The other two were protected. A man outside in a car and a man inside the house. I checked them out completely. Then I called Josh Fishbein. We talked a while, and he couldn't wait to tell me about his protection. He was taking it all as a lark. If I'd tried either one of the other two, I would have been blown away."

"I found the same thing. So now we try something else. I don't know what. I'll let you hear if I need you."

"Hey, I'm running short."

"I thought you might be." He took out his billfold and handed her ten new hundred-dollar bills. Then, without another word, he went out the back door, through the empty lot behind her house and around to his car. Despite the pain pills, his shoulder hurt like hell.

By morning Ackors had his plan. He made a telephone call and talked directly with Willy Lockhart. "Willy, I have a small job for you. It's worth a thousand dollars, cash, half now and half when the work is done. Interested?"

"Hell, you know I am. And for that money, it damned well ain't legal, but who gives a shit? What do I do?"

Willy and Ackors worked all morning setting it up. Willy provided the pick-up, stolen, and Ackors dug up the rest of the dynamite from a ranch he used.

At last they had it ready, a pick-up loaded with 40 cases of 60-percent dynamite. The entire front bumper was rigged as an impact detonator, but this time it had a switch on it. With the switch off, you could use the bumper to ram into things, but with it on, it acted as a detonator for the whole load.

The plan was for Willy to drive to the area, get through the guards, tie down the steering wheel, and aim the pick-up at Building 176 and jump. When he hit, Willy would run like hell.

"After the bomb goes off, there'll be so much confusion, you'll be able to walk right out that hole in the fence without anyone looking at you twice."

Willy scowled. He didn't like it. The driving he could do, and he could blast the guard if he had to with no sweat, but being so close to that kind of a bomb. . . . He shrugged. What the hell, a guy only lives once.

"I'm ready," he said. "When do we move?"

They set it for four o'clock, just at the shift change at the Labs, when there always was lots of activity and some confusion. That also was when the guards still had an hour to go on their shift and they would be tired.

Ackors drove along the outer fence of the Labs that afternoon to where he could see the open space around the big warehouse Building 176. Then he waited. He knew that was where the trucks that carried the betatron were stored. The big machine wasn't moved off the low-boy trailer. Knock that out, and they would need a year to replace it. That would carry a lot of weight with Mr. Smith.

Down in the Labs, Mark had just finished talking with Dr. Dessel. The director had ordered all the scientists working on the LONG REACH program to live in the facility for the next week. Mark had smiled when he heard choppers dropping in from the sky that morning. Three of the big double-rotor Sikorskys came in, and each disgorged 20 combat-ready Marines. The detail had come in from Camp Pendleton in California on a special exercise. Mark drifted up just as a stern-jawed first lieutenant assembled his troops in a driveway and gave them the word.

"This exercise is over. Now the work begins. You all will be issued live ammo when this formation breaks. All weapons, including the MGs and rocket launchers will be operational twenty-four hours a day. We go on a twelve-hour shift as of now. Officially this is an exercise for emergency interior guard duty."

He paused and his eyes lit up, and then Mark remembered where he had seen the man before. He was a 'Nam vet Mark had served with on several raids, and a good man.

"Unofficially, this is a top-secret installation," the Marine continued. "There has been a great deal of sabotage here. We are a defensive force, and we must hold this position and stop the problem. You'll be deployed soon. We're primarily defending one big building, number 176, and if anyone tries to enter that building by force, or without authorization, we capture or shoot to kill. Is that clear? Squad leaders report."

Mark drifted away. At least now they had some professional security.

That afternoon at four, the guard at the outer parking lot entrance to the secure area watched a pick-up roll to his gate and stop. Before the guard could say a word, the driver lifted a silenced .45 and shot the guard in the head, driving him back into the small guard box. Then the pick-up moved on through the gate.

The first alarm came at the second security gate, when the pick-up slammed through the wire. A Marine jumped up from his position behind the security box and sent a dozen rounds from his M-14 into the truck, but all of the rounds struck the cardboard boxes holding the dynamite, which did not explode.

The truck continued undamaged. Willy had a determined look on his face now. He drove a quarter of a mile, then turned left and toward the outer edge of the complex, where he could see the big warehouse, Building 176, where the betatron was stored. He'd been there before. This was where he had wrecked the two diesel engines.

Willy saw a guard post and drove around it, then angled back toward the building. Willy knew he was in trouble when he spotted three men in Marine green fatigues run out, flop down, and begin firing at him. He flipped the switch on the dash, activating the front bumper as a detonator on the pick-up. Three slugs hit the side of the pick-up, and another one shattered the back window. For a moment he thought of riding the truck into the wall, going out in a blaze of glory.

He heard a loudspeaker.

"This facility is a hundred percent under guard. Stop or you will be fired upon."

He got within a hundred yards of the big building, then aimed the truck, tied down the steering wheel with a stretch hook cord, and pushed the 10 pounds of plumbers lead over toward the gas pedal.

Then he saw the dozen Marines rush around the corner of the building. A Jeep followed them. Willy panicked. The son of a bitch didn't tell him he'd have to fight the whole goddamned U.S. Marine Corps! Furiously he pushed the lead on the gas pedal and slid to the far side, ready to jump. The pick-up was rolling along at about 40 m.p.h. when he was ready. He had just reached for the door handle when the whole side of the pick-up seemed to erupt toward him. There was a thunderous explosion that sucked every bit of air from his lungs as an M-47 Dragon missile went off and struck the side of the pick-up near the engine. Willy was vaguely conscious as he hung half out the pick-up window. Shrapnel, body metal, and glass fragments had torn into his head, neck, and chest, and he screamed into the fury of the explosion. He was still alive when the second Dragon missile fired by the Marines hit the tauplin-covered boxes of dynamite in the pick-up box. The whole load exploded with a belching, gut-shattering cacophony as the 40 cases of dynamite erupted into a huge fireball and blasted the truck into irregular components, propelling the front wheels and engine within inches of the big building.

One of Willy Lockhart's legs fell 15 feet from the missile-firing Jeep. A hand sailed to the very top of the warehouse roof and landed on the rock and tar covering. The smoking rear wheels of the pick-up, their tires burning furiously, had been blasted a block away and were still rolling.

On the Jeep a hundred yards north, Sgt. Oscar Wonderland patted the Dragon missile launcher and watched the cloud of smoke where the pick-up had once been.

"Jesus H. Christ!" A PFC Marine on the missile team whispered as he watched the remains of the pick-up and wondered what had happened to the driver.

Sgt. Wonderland calmly ordered the Dragon missile launcher reloaded and nodded at his team. "Welcome to combat."

Chapter 13

THE LAST GRENADE

It was nearly six o'clock that evening before Dr. Dessel, Mark, and the FBI men had assessed the damage. They had a squad of Marines pick up as much of the truck driver as they could find. There was no identification yet. His smashed and badly burned head had been found two blocks away. The Marines zipped up the body bag and put it in an ambulance.

Now all four men sat in the director's office.

"There was no damage to the betatron, and no harm done to the buildings or the heavy trucks, but we did lose almost forty windows," Dr. Dessel said.

"We were lucky," Sanchez added. "Damned lucky again."

"From now on, we will have heavy trucks blocking both on-site road gates. Everyone coming or going will have a complete inspection, and only authorized vehicles will be permitted. A squad of six Marines will be on duty at each gate for the next week."

"Good," Mark said. "That sounds like some security that will do some good."

"It was Lt. Baker's idea, I'm afraid," Dr. Dessel said. "He indicated this was the only way he would continue to maintain his troops at the facility."

Howard Goodman stood and walked around the office. "I guess that takes care of this case. We'll file a final report to our office, but it's my guess that we nailed the brains behind all this. It was that damn suicide mission. That pick-up run today was a lulu. How could anybody talk somebody else into doing anything like that?"

They said good night and left. Sanchez and Mark went for dinner, leaving Goodman to play with his Penetrator files. Then Mark drove back to the motel and found Joanna on the phone to Washington. She was deeply involved in a report to Dan Griggs. Mark kissed her on the cheek and said he'd be back soon. He had one more lead to check out. She wrote a note that he damn well better be back soon, and kissed him good-bye.

Mark still didn't think it was over. Somehow the brains behind everything, and perhaps an enemy agent, was still out there on the streets, still plotting. Mark was down to one lead, Dawna Lane. She hadn't been involved in the hit today, at least not openly. Mark drove past her house and found the front room lights on. He parked half a block down and walked back to a spot where he could see both Dawna's front and side doors. Then he settled down to wait. It might be a futile try, but it was all he had left. As far as he knew, the girl might think he had left town after killing her man in the over-the-cliff game.

About an hour after he had hidden beside the hedge, someone went up to the front door. Mark watched closely but found it was only a teenager collecting for the paper. He took his money and rode his bike away.

It was fully dark now, and Mark moved closer, finding another vantage point just inside the fence bordering her property. No one was home next door, and he sat on the far side of the fence, watching cars and viewing the whole scene through a long crack between boards.

By ten o'clock, he had about given up hope. Then he heard the phone ring inside Dawna's house. She answered it, and a few minutes later turned off the side porch light. Mark wondered why, and found out in five minutes when a short, rotund man came across the back lot, edged around the corner of the house, and slid quickly inside through the side door.

Mark could not see his face, but the shape and size were easy to recognize. The only person associated with this case who fit that description was the savings-and-loan man, Ackors. He was the one who introduced Dr. Dessel at that little ceremony.

Ackors? Mark waited a few minutes more, then moved to the near side of the house and tried to look in the windows. The drapes had been drawn in the living room. No other lights were on except in the kitchen. Ackors—yes it had to be he who was the spy. What a beautiful cover. It was hard to lose money in the savings-and-loan business. Ackors could hire the men to run the firm for him and be a figurehead, with lots of time for charities to cover up for his spying and dirty work.

Mark ran silently to Dawna's side door, listened carefully, and tried the knob. It was unlocked. He stepped inside and through a small entryway, then heard someone coming. Quickly he edged open another door. This one led to the garage. He stepped inside.

Both Dawna and Ackors went to the side door. "Stay out of this part. I may need you in a hurry. I don't know how much more of this I can manage and maintain my cover. If I have to travel, you'll go with me."

"We'll see, Harry. I like it here."

"You'll like it anywhere, woman. If I say go, you'll go. I know where the bodies are buried, remember?"

"And that would bury you too, don't forget that. You push me under, and I'm damn well pulling you along with me. Don't forget that, fat little man!"

He left, slamming the door. She laughed.

"You fat slob. You think you own me?" She screamed it at the side door, stared after him a moment, then went to the kitchen.

Mark came out of the garage and moved silently toward the kitchen. When he eased the door open, she was mixing a drink.

"Hello, Dawna Lane. I'm the one you didn't kill, remember?"

She looked up, and only for a second did the shock show on her face; then she smiled.

"Yes, of course, the cute one with black eyes and peroxided hair. The Justice Department snoop. How could I forget. You're not very nice, pouring your drink on my carpet. I finally found the wet spot when my man didn't come back. That really wasn't very neighborly of you."

He watched her hands. They stayed quietly in plain sight on the counter. She made no move toward the rack of knives nearby. Mark felt no need to draw his .45.

"A few things I don't understand," Mark said. "I know you killed the first one, Mahon—knocked him out and pushed the car down the cliff. Simple. But the next one, Duyck. Was that a mistake? You must have shot him out of anger or fear and then had to try to make it look like a solo job. Suicide with no powder burns is always a tough one, but you tried. The pillow bit to deaden the sound so the neighbors wouldn't get upset—you could have done better than that. Besides, Duyck wasn't the suicide type."

"The police have gone over all of that with me, and they've seen no reason to charge me."

"Not yet. I'm filling in the local sheriff on some of your finer qualities."

"I don't suppose you'd want a drink?"

"Not even coffee, not yours."

"That's a shame. I have some very good Scotch."

"Help yourself. You know I hadn't pegged Mr. Public-Minded Citizen Harry Ackors as the real villain in this little drama. He's the undercover agent, and you're his sexy right hand, among other parts."

"You don't have to get nasty." She smiled as she said it and began unbuttoning her blouse. He could see the nipples pushing against the tight fabric as they grew rigid. She let the blouse hang open, the sides of her breasts glowing brownly from her all-over suntan.

"I mean, we don't have to fight, you and I. I'm not into politics. I much prefer men, and you certainly are a man, one great big chunk of a man. What do you think?"

She slid the blouse off her shoulders and let it fall to the floor. Her suntanned breasts rose even more as she straightened and walked toward him.

"Well, can't you say anything? You have seen a girl before."

"Who does Harry Ackors work for, the Russians?"

Her hands had been at her sides as she walked. Now her eyes flared with anger, and her right hand came up, throwing a small knife underhanded. It must have been in her waistband. Mark had been ready, wondering when she would make her first move. He had to dodge backward and to his right, and that gave her room to slip past him and run into the living room. He was right behind her, but from somewhere she had grabbed a foot-long knife and turned, charging directly back at him.

Mark sidestepped and tripped her as she slashed. The long blade caught his shirt front, slicing through the cloth, then tearing free as she fell.

She hit on her hands and knees but was up like a cat, her bare breasts swaying from the motion.

Dawna drove for a cushion on the sofa, but Mark pushed her away and got to it. Underneath he found a .25 automatic. As he claimed it, she reversed direction and pulled a .38 revolver from under the matching chair. Mark rolled over the back of the sofa as she fired. The round buried itself in the frame.

Mark edged around the couch at floor level and looked over the room. She had vanished. He checked again and found an inch of her round bottom in the white pants showing behind the big chair.

"That's one," Mark said. "Remember to count your shots—and mine. I've got seven in the magazine and one in the chamber."

"You bastard! All I'll need is one."

"Not the way you shoot." Mark slipped his shoe off and threw it to the other side of the room. She raised up and fired three times at the noise before she realized he had tricked her.

"That's four. And I bet all your spare rounds are in your blouse pocket."

"Bastard."

Mark saw the nose of her revolver come over the

back of the big chair. He couldn't figure it out until he looked over his head and saw a heavy plate glass mirror. It was 6 feet long and 4 feet wide. A round would shatter . . . Before he could surge out of the way, she fired and the mirror exploded, raining down on him hundreds of slivers and some larger pieces that could cut his leg or arm to the bone. Mark dodged the avalanche, rolling furiously from side to side to avoid as much of the falling glass as he could. When he saw the last of it fall, he expected the girl to be standing over him and sighting in with her revolver.

Instead she ran for the kitchen. He leaped up, brushed off the shards, and made a cautious but tactical advance. She wasn't in the kitchen. Around the corner he saw the door to the garage close slowly. She had to be in there. He turned out the lights in the hallway, then went through the garage door low and fast, ramming into a stack of cardboard boxes that crashed to the floor.

A voice laughed from the darkness. "Now we're on more equal terms. I had a box of .38 shells out here, and now I have plenty of rounds instead of just one."

"Just don't catch a bad chest cold."

"Bastard!"

"I've no intention of killing you."

"Good, that will make it easier for me to blow you away, to blow your ass into hell, you Justice Department snoop."

"Why?"

"You know too damn much."

"So you did kill Mahon, and you shot Duyck when he got suspicious of your probing questions."

"Yeah, so what? It won't do you any good. Even if you aren't a hick town cop."

"Neither is Sheriff Logan."

"He's wired. I've been sleeping with him for six months."

"Anybody in town you don't bang?"

"Yeah, the mayor and you."

Since he had first turned off the lights in the hall, Mark had been working up his *Sho-tu-ca* night sight powers. He had learned the old Cheyenne Dog Soldier technique after many months of instruction and training by medicine man David Red Eagle back at the Stronghold in California. With it he could see as well in a coal mine at midnight as most people can when dusk is beginning to fall.

Until he had it in force, he relied on his sensitive hearing. She moved to his left. He threw his other shoe to the right, and the noise brought two shots from her revolver. Mark fired low in relation to the flashes, barely making out her crouched form.

Her scream billowed through the garage.

"Fucking bastard!" she screamed. "Don't gloat, I fell for it and you got in a lucky one. But I'll live, and I've got a surprise you'll really get a bang out of."

Mark concentrated on his night sight, and as he did, she became clear. She had been hit in the lower leg by his round, and she was wrapping a cloth around it. Lying on the floor near her was an old-fashioned M-3 fragger grenade, the pineapple kind with spoon handle, ring, and pull pin.

The Penetrator knew he had a problem. He wanted the girl alive to testify against Ackors, but if he didn't do something quickly, they both could be dead. Those old grenades became touchy and unstable after being stored for so long. That one was probably over 20 years old. They could do strange things; some even exploded as soon as the safety pin was pulled. He could shoot her hand when she reached for the grenade, but she picked it up before he could sight in and she turned. He didn't know if she had pulled the pin or not.

He had to wait. She turned back and she did pull the pin, but held the spoon tightly against the bomb as she wrapped some binder twine cord around it. She edged toward the automatic washing machine and got behind it. Then she laughed. That was when he knew what she was going to do.

Mark fired into the side of the washer. One of her legs was showing, and she pulled it back and laughed again.

"I'm gonna get you good, bastard. Geet your ass good!"

Mark watched her arm come out and roll the grenade in his direction. The fuzzy binder twine unwound as the grenade rolled toward Mark until there were only two wraps left. Mark looked for something to shield himself. There was nothing! He judged the distance to the small side door. Fifteen feet—no way he could make it!

He flattened himself on the cement, turned his head away, and put both hands over his neck. Nothing happened. He looked again. His night sight showed him that the fuzzy binder twine had crisscrossed and hung up. It wouldn't unroll the rest of the way. The grenade wasn't armed yet. He saw her tug at the string, pull gently, jerk it to try to free it. She had no way of knowing what had gone wrong. The twine still was tangled and wouldn't unwind.

She pulled the string harder, and the grenade moved a foot back toward her. Dawna began to cry.

"Goddammit, work, you stinking son of a bitch!"

Mark crawled toward the side door that he hoped opened to the yard.

"Work!" she screamed.

He was near the door now when he saw her jerk the binder twine hard. The cord slipped free and unrolled, but the force of the pull reversed the direction of the grenade. The string fell off, the spoon popped off, and the bomb was armed—only now it was rolling on the flat cement floor back toward Dawna's hiding spot. Mark came off the floor in a charge, hit the flimsy wooden door with his shoulder, and took off half the outside molding as the door splintered outward. He fell to the backyard grass and rolled away.

A second later the grenade went off inside the garage with a shattering *karump*. Smoke gushed from the door. Mark got to his feet and rushed back in, fighting the acrid smoke and dust. He found the light switch and pushed it on. Oddly, the flying shrapnel had missed the bulb.

Dawna Lane lay slumped behind the washing machine against the firewall. The grenade must have been almost on top of her before it went off. Her face was a pulpy mass of bleeding, shredded flesh; only one eye was recognizable. Her nose was gone, her cheeks only raw ribbons of exposed tissue, her throat and breasts riddled with hundreds of small splinters of shrapnel.

The unstable grenade had shattered into thousands of small shards of iron instead of blasting into killing-sized chunks as it had been designed to do.

Dawna wasn't dead. Her right hand and arm were

untouched. With a supreme effort, she lifted her head and stared at Mark with her one good eye.

"Kill me!" she pleaded. The words came out slurred and hard to understand. "Shoot me, bastard. Please finish me quickly!" She reached toward him with her hand.

Mark hit the magazine release on the .45, caught the metal carrier, and handed the weapon to her. It had one live round in the chamber ready to fire. She followed his action and his logic. This way she couldn't shoot him and then herself. As Mark gave her the weapon, he stepped away behind the washer, not for his own protection, but to give her this one last moment alone. It's the way he would want it for himself if it ever came to that.

Dawna Lane thanked him silently, looked at the .45, and made sure the safety was off. Then she lifted the heavy weapon until she could see the round black hole of the muzzle with her one good eye and pulled the trigger.

Chapter 14

ONCE BURNED, TWICE DEAD

Mark took the .45 from the dead woman's hand, wiped the metal free of her blood, then turned off the lights in the garage and eased out the back door. He squatted in the darkness, watching the surrounding yards. Nothing moved. Evidently nobody had heard the grenade go off or hadn't bothered to investigate. The Penetrator walked through the vacant back lot to the next street and around to his car.

There was nothing more he could do tonight. Ackors was the target, but he had no way to prove it. Sheriff Logan would demand proof. Mark couldn't even tell the sheriff yet that the man of the year in Los Alamos was really a spy, a Russian agent. Proof was what Mark had to find, and find fast.

Joanna Tabler was waiting for him when he went back to the motel. She wore a frilly blue nylon shortie nightgown. He had forgotten how strikingly beautiful she was. She smiled and held out her arms and kissed him without saying a word. They sat on the bed, and he began to relax as she undressed him.

Joanna was exactly the medicine that Mark needed.

Much later, in the early morning hours, he told her about Dawna Lane and how she had died. Joanna cried.

The next morning Mark was at the Labs at 7:30, waiting for the director. Early that morning Mark had phoned in an anonymous tip to the sheriff's office, reporting that he'd heard an explosion and screaming from the garage at 197 Cactus Street. That was where Dawna lived. He hung up before they could ask who he was.

Howard Goodman arrived as Mark waited and packed up his Penetrator files.

"Going back to D.C., Zilke. This damn job is done. The case is officially closed. The brains of the outfit blew himself up in that pick-up in one last grandstand play. We both know it, so why the hell should we waste the taxpayers' money messing around?"

He snapped his briefcase closed and held out his hand.

"Hell, it hasn't been a lot of fun, but you seem to get things done, Zilke. We might meet again sometime." Mark shook his hand, then Goodman went to the door. "Oh hell. Almost forgot. That Marine, Lt. Baker, told me to say good-bye for him. I talked to Washington last night and told them to pull the Marines out of here, that we don't need them anymore. They got in their choppers this morning just before sun-up and hauled ass. Hey, Zilke, I got to catch a plane. If you hear anything new about that bastard, the Penetrator, let me know."

Then Goodman was gone. Evidently so were the Marines. Mark knew the case wasn't over. He set his jaw and stared at the closed door. Goodman had sent away the Marines. Now was the time when they were needed the most. Mark drove to the bivouac area the leathernecks had used, but the pup tents were all gone, the area had been policed, and it was hard to tell that 60 Marines had camped there.

Back at the director's office, Mark slumped in a chair.

"The Marines are gone," Mark said.

"Yes, Mr. Goodman seemed to think . . ."

"Goodman is an idiot. This thing isn't over. What do you know about Harry Ackors?"

"Everything. He's a friend. I've worked with him for seven years on community projects. He's a fine man."

"Wrong, Dr. Dessel. He's a sadistic killer, an enemy of this country. He's been using your friendship for the past seven years to steal classified and secret information from the Labs and is passing it along. He's a professional Russian intelligence agent, and right now his job is to stop the LONG REACH program any way that he can. He's the cause of all of your problems here."

Dr. Dessel jumped up shouting. "No, no! That just can't be! He's the best friend I have. Just the night before last he saved me from . . ." The scientist stopped.

"Go on, Dr. Dessel. He saved you from what?"

Dr. Dessel sat down at his desk, his eyes half closed, his hand on his forehead. Then quietly, precisely, he told Mark exactly what had happened. His memory was coming back, and he remembered he had a telephone call from Dawna Lane. She told him she knew he didn't like her, but this was more important than any personalities or petty bickering. She said she had something vital to tell him about Operation LONG REACH, and she had to do it right then, that night, before she lost her nerve.

He remembered with scientific precision everything

that happened to him after he woke up in the motel room. Mark absorbed it all.

"And then Ackors got you awake and dressed and said he'd take care of it all, am I right? He said he would dispose of the dead girl and cover it up with the motel operator, that you were a gifted and important man and that she was just a prostitute."

"Yes, that's almost all of it. How did you know that?"

"Dr. Dessel, it's a trick as old as men themselves. But usually it doesn't involve murder. Are you sure the girl was really dead?"

"Oh, yes. Nobody could live after what had been done to her."

"And you still think you did it?"

"I can't be certain that I didn't do it. I've never been violence-prone before. . . ."

"Dr. Dessel, forget it. You were tricked, set up, conned. First they doped whatever you drank at her house. Then they got you to the motel and stripped you. Then Ackors tortured the girl and killed her. He was ready when you were about due to come out of the drug."

"Why? . . . Oh, my God! That night I told Harry that I'd do just absolutely anything for him. I said I'd always be in his debt."

"Just where he wants you. The blackmail on the next big program would be his coming action. Ackors thinks ahead."

"What can I do now?" Dr. Dessel asked.

"Forget it right now. Later you can report it to the sheriff. Ackors isn't through yet with Operation LONG REACH. He needs a big strike, a heavy blow, something that might damage the betatron, put him in a better light with his Russian superiors.

That's why I wish the Marines hadn't left. He's desperate now. The weapon works, all you have to do now is down-size it, right?"

"Essentially, yes. The weapon, for all practical purposes, is developed. But now we must adapt and adjust it to a specific use."

"So now we protect it. I'd suggest you put your guards back on full alert and twelve-hour shifts. Get half of them on duty today, and use them for exterior guard duty around the buildings where the vital LONG REACH components are stored."

"Yes, yes, that sounds reasonable. I'll talk to Wilbur right away." Dr. Dessel paused and looked at the ceiling. "Zilke, are you sure, sure about the motel and that girl? Sure I didn't do it?"

"Yes, knowing what's gone on before, I'm a hundred-percent sure that you're not a killer, not a man who could torture a young girl. I'm also one hundred-percent sure that Harry Ackors is an enemy agent trying to stop LONG REACH. If he did this big favor for you out of the goodness of his heart, I'd be skeptical. You're not that kind of man who would enjoy carving up a girl while having sex with her at the same time. Ackors probably would enjoy it tremendously."

"How terrible!" He thought for a moment. "Mr. Zilke, you are probably right, and I am relieved . . ."

"Dr. Dessel, I'm glad you told me. Now let's get those guards set up and seal off that area as tightly as you can."

Outside Mark watched the security go around Building 176. There were eight guards on the big warehouse. All the men had pistols. Mark wished they all had M-14 rifles. At least that way they would have some stopping power with the .30-caliber slug. He toured the area again, then went in to talk about the weapons.

Dr. Dessel was understanding.

"Yes, I know the weapons aren't long range, but we're in a city situation here. Much of our complex is inside the city limits. The city council requested that our guards not use rifles because of the danger. Rifles would mean a much higher problem for civilians around the Labs and in the city."

"But do you have any rifles for emergencies?"

"Well, yes. But I'm afraid they haven't been used for years."

Dr. Dessel told the security chief to let Mark look at the weapons. Mark grinned when he saw them. Nothing to write home about, that was for sure: two army M-1s, the old reliable, and a .30-06 sniper rifle, all Korean war surplus from the 1950s, he guessed.

"Any ammo?"

"Yes, we have some here someplace."

"Find it. I'm going to field strip these and see if I can get them working. Do you have any cleaning gear?"

A half-hour later, Mark had both the M-1s torn down, wiped off, oiled, and put back together. Both functioned perfectly. He loaded a dozen clips for the M-1s with eight rounds in a clip, and then went to work on the .30-06. The extractor was broken, and the weapon could not fire. He put it back on the shelf and took the two M-1s out to the guards at the big building. Two of the men claimed army experience and had fired the M-1s. Mark gave each man six clips of ammo, with the orders to load and lock. He went back to his car hoping for the best.

Mark had just parked outside the administration

office when he heard the whirring of a small helicopter. At first he didn't sense any alarm. Then he realized he hadn't heard a chopper around Los Alamos since the Marines had arrived. Were they coming back?

He looked up and saw the chopper coming in low from the north. It was barely over the trees, a blue and white bird. It circled the Labs complex once, then came back toward the cafeteria. It was first-shift lunch time, and a dozen picnic tables set up outside were half full of workers.

Suddenly two small black objects dropped from the aircraft, and Mark broke into a run toward the tables, his .45 out and ready. He thought the black blobs might be hand grenades. It was an actual bombing attack!

The first two grenades went off 100 feet in the air and north of the tables. Mark snapped a shot at the chopper, knowing he was well out of range, but he fired once and ran on. The whirlybird dropped lower this time, so the four-second fuse train of the grenades wouldn't set off the bomb too high. The next small bomb went off 15 feet in the air, spraying the ground with deadly shrapnel, but this time the bomb was too far south.

A dozen people left their lunch and ran toward the cafeteria building. Others stared in amazement. The pilot made a small circle and came back at what Mark guessed was 400 feet. Mark was almost at the cafeteria now.

"Get under the tables," he screamed at them, and half the people still there dove for the protection of the wooden tabletops. A few more ran, and eight or ten stood, open mouthed and unable to take any action at all.

Mark blasted again with the .45, estimating the 400-foot range as being a little far for an effective hit, but it might cause the pilot some second thoughts. The defensive action gave him some satisfaction.

Two more grenades fell, and Mark saw that these would be on target at the end of the line of tables. Mark flattened himself on the grass and heard both bombs go off with the typical crackling roar of the old pineapples. At once screams erupted. Mark ran toward the chopper and emptied his .45 at it, then turned to the injured. The helicopter made one more tight circle, turned, and flew to the north just over the trees.

The Labs ambulance was there before Mark had found all of the wounded. One man in his twenties was dying. He had taken two heavy pieces of shrapnel in his chest and another in his neck. One woman was seriously hit in the back, but was in no danger. Eleven others had bleeding wounds.

Mark helped them load the two serious cases, and the ambulance rushed off for the city hospital. The walking wounded were taken in private cars to the doctors.

Mark stood there berating himself. Why hadn't he kept one of the M-1s himself? He could have picked the pilot's eyes out with a trusty M-1, even if he had to waste the first few rounds sighting it in on the blue target.

The Penetrator went to the warehouse and took one of the M-1s from the guard. The man said the rifle was too heavy anyway.

Back in the director's office, Dr. Dèssel looked drawn and shaken. "That's the first man we've had die here in a long time," the director said. "I'm sure he'll die—he was very bad off."

"Why don't you close down for the rest of the day?" Mark said. "It's Friday, you'll only lose half a day. No one is going to get any work done from now on anyway. And it will make this place a lot easier to protect. And put a request in for them to send back some Marines. We may need them if we don't get this cleared up quickly. We sure as hell could have used those Marines about an hour ago. Also have the sheriff see if he can find out who flew that chopper. It must have come from your airport here."

Mark stormed out of the office and found a phone. He called Joanna at the motel and told her to check on the helicopters in the area and at the airport. He wanted to find out how many choppers there were for hire. He said he'd call her back in an hour.

The rest of the afternoon, Mark prowled the deserted complex. All of the workers had gone home. All of the security guards were there on an overlapping shift. He marched along the fence, then criss-crossed the area in his car. For a while he walked the post around the betatron storage Building 176.

When he called Joanna about four o'clock, she had bad news.

"Four different outfits rent choppers at the local airport. It's a private plane only type of strip. They use the choppers for surveys and some crop dusting. One guy has lessons and regular rentals for pilots trying to get in their required hours for a chopper rating."

"Four. Okay, we may have to check them out

later. One dropped some grenades on the facility this noon."

"It's on the radio. That one boy did die, but the others will be all right."

"Good. I'll be down here at the Labs all night.

"Anything I can do?"

He grinned. "Just rest. We'll have a lot of time to catch up when this one is all over."

By 8:30 that evening, nothing had happened. It was fully dark. Mark had raided the cafeteria and built himself a torpedo sandwich and found a quart of milk. He ate as he walked around the buildings.

It was nearly midnight when Mark spotted someone at the end of one of the lab buildings. Mark ran up silently and saw the man working at a valve at the side of the structure.

Mark was within 20 feet of the intruder when the man whirled and fired a handgun. The round missed. Mark returned fire with the M-1 putting a big slug through the man's forehead.

He ran up and saw that the man had been working on a gas line valve. It was in the open position, and the handle and stem had been broken off.

Mark smelled the gas at once. He forced in a window, and gas began to rush out. The building must be filled with the volatile stuff, and there was more coming in all the time, with no way to turn it off.

Two security guards heard Mark's shot and rushed up to help.

"Get to security and maintenance and tell them to shut off the gas in the whole complex. This leak has to be stopped."

The two men left on the run.

Mark backed away from the building. Now gas

was seeping from around the windows and doors. He coughed and moved back another 20 yards. There was nothing he could do but wait and hope.

Three minutes after Mark found the gas, and precisely at midnight by Mark's digital watch, he heard the chopper again. It sounded like the same one he had seen that afternoon. It came in from the north with no lights, and Mark had a hard time finding it in the black sky. Mark pushed the safety on the M-1 to the off position and waited.

Behind the gas-filled building, Mark saw a red flare go off. It was probably a fusee flare, the kind people carry in their cars. It was not dangerous. But a flare like that could quickly identify a target. The chopper turned and came straight for the flare.

Mark worked up his *Sho-tu-ca* night sight. He'd been using it all evening, but now he concentrated on it more, and as he did, he saw the helicopter with the small door open. The pilot leaned out and looked down, then brought his bird in lower.

Mark waited until the chopper was as low as he thought it would come, about 300 feet over the roofs, then Mark began firing. He could see the .30-caliber slugs digging into the light metal of the helicopter. They didn't seem to affect it.

One of his rounds went into the pilot's shoulder, and the machine lurched crazily for a moment, then steadied. Something dropped from the aircraft.

Was it a grenade? No, too large. A bomb? That's when he remembered that the building was filled with explosive gas. The whole structure was one huge bomb, 80 feet long and 40 feet wide!

The package exploded on impact 50 feet from the target. It went off with a resounding roar, but Mark hardly noticed it. He was jamming another clip into his M-1 and sighting in on the chopper. It came closer this time, and Mark fired into the canopy, going for the pilot. Another bomb fell from the chopper's open door. It went straight and true and hit just outside the gas-filled building.

The blast of the small bomb could not be distinguished from the tremendous shattering, belching, *karumphing* roar that followed at once. The sky lit up for half a mile around, and Mark felt himself blasted a dozen feet backward and slammed to the ground like a matchstick in a tornado. He felt all of the oxygen sucked out of his lungs to fuel the blast. He had time only to look up and saw the helicopter trying to maneuver away. But some of his shots into the engine had done their damage, and the bird could not lift away. It was in the direct path when the first soaring firecloud touched the chopper. The fuel in the tank exploded, and Mark saw the craft blast into pieces and fall to a street 100 yards from the fiercely burning building in front of him.

He knew he had to get back. Mark was crawling away when the second explosion tore through the lab structure, and he sensed the searing, blinding, white-hot light that tortured his skin, that blurred his vision through closed eyes and crumpled him back to the ground. Then the blackness that was blessed unconsciousness closed in around him.

EPILOGUE

Mark felt strong hands holding him down as he came out of the mist of unconsciousness. For just a moment he had a marvelous dreaming feeling of total comfort, of softly welcome, unreal bliss.

Then his face hurt like fire and he moaned.

"He's starting to come out of it."

He didn't know who was talking or why, or where he was. And for a moment he didn't even care who he was. Then the burning flooded back, his nerve endings shrilled a chorus of complaints, and his body let out a long, hissing breath.

That was when he realized that he couldn't see, that he couldn't even open his eyes. Everything was deep gray, not night black, but an unnerving gray that made him think of death.

"Keith, Keith Zilke, can you hear me? This is Joanna. It's time to wake up now."

He felt her take his hand and squeeze it, and he pressed back.

Mark tried to sit up, but again the strong hands held him down. Then he realized they weren't hands, they were straps. He was in a bed, and he was strapped down, and the last thing he remembered was that secondary explosion. . . .

"Joanna?" The voice sounded strange, but it was his. His tongue didn't work quite right.

"Yes, I'm right here. You're in the Labs medical ward, and you're lucky you aren't fried as crisp as four-minute bacon. You had me so worried, I nearly tore this place apart before they let me inside. It took a call to Dan Griggs to get me here." She kept talking, and he had the idea that if she stopped, she would start crying from relief or pleasure or something he couldn't define. She rambled on.

"So I finally got in, and they let me sit with you. They strapped you down so you wouldn't roll over and mess up the bandages on your face. They say you've got a sunburn that won't stop. It's something that was in the building that blew up, something they are working on that they won't talk about. But they say it is only a first-degree burn, and they wanted to put some special medication on it for two days. Then you'll be free to leave, and you'll be good as new in two weeks—they think.

"Evidently they don't understand everything about this project, and they want to see what happens to you. So I told Dan when I had him on the phone that you were hurt and I needed two weeks off, and he said impossible, so I quit and he said, 'You quit again?' So I told him of course. It's been over a year since I quit the last time, and I haven't had a vacation since then, and if he didn't like it . . ." She laughed. "Do you think I'm talking too much?"

"Yes."

"Good. Oh, the doctor is here. He wants to unwrap you and then you can take a look at your sunburn. Right, Doctor?"

"Miss Tabler, if you will move back and give me a little room, we'll see how our patient is coming along."

"Oh, Dr. Marshall, this is Keith Zilke. Keith, Dr. Marshall."

"Great," Mark said. He felt the cold scissors slide along his cheek and the fabric part. When the last of the white gauze came off his face a few moments later, he blinked in surprise at the intensity of the light. He closed his eyes again.

"Yes, I was afraid of that. Your eyeballs have been burned too, but only marginally. You'll need a week here, I'm afraid, before I can release you."

It was ten minutes before Mark could open his eyes and keep them open. He was sitting up then and using Tabler's sunglasses. He found he could stand the light in the dimmed room. Mark's face looked as if it belonged to a red rock cod just up from 80 fathoms.

"Don't worry, young man, this will pass. We've had one case like it before, and there don't seem to be any lasting effects."

"Wait a minute, Doctor. You said there doesn't *seem* to be any ill effects. You don't really know what you're dealing with here, then, do you?"

The doctor ignored the question. "Your eyes will adjust to the light gradually, and within a week or two you'll be back to normal. Wear sunglasses whenever you want to."

"Is it radiation burn?"

"I really can't tell you."

The doctor put a new coating of the ointment on Mark's face, then left the room.

Joanna picked up with her running commentary. "So H. R. Rivers was charged with six counts this morning in federal district court in Santa Fe. One of them is murder, which she shares with four others who used the weapons. All nineteen of the group have been charged with something, and bail money has been set so high that all are still in jail. It looks as if H. R. Rivers and her brand of head-busting ecology are through. She finally admitted that someone paid her ten thousand dollars to come here and demonstrate. When the district attorney pushed her, she admitted that the man's name was Ackors and that she picked up the money through Dawna Lane. She was working this ecology protest strictly for the cash involved."

"What about Ackors? Was that him in the chopper?"

Joanna smiled grimly. "It was. They identified him by dental charts, even though some of his fillings were melted right out of his teeth. They had to work with cavities where fillings used to be, but they know it was him. The New Mexico Aircraft Company rented the chopper to him at noon, and he never brought it back. He flew off in it, they are sure of that, and paid for the flight in advance. We don't have to worry about Harry Ackors anymore."

"No, but his shadow agent will move in and take over and carry on. He or she is probably picking up the pieces of Ackors' organization right now."

"Somebody else can worry about them."

"I hope so. Tell these jokers I can't stay here for a week. Tell them I have to be in Los Angeles on an assignment. Get me out of here in two days, or too many people are going to start asking questions, official questions."

Joanna had never seen Mark so tense.

Three days later, they were in a small motel right on the sand in Laguna Beach. Mark stretched out on the king-sized bed and watched the waves breaking on a rocky point.

"No one knows we're here?"

"No one. In three more days, the last of the

special salve goes on your face and hands, and then your burns will be nearly healed. All I have to do is check in with that doctor, and if he says so, we'll get some kind of a test made on you. That's it."

"Any idea what that second explosion was all about?"

She shook her head. "I asked the director. I told Dr. Dessel that he owed you that much. He said it wasn't connected with the LONG REACH program, and that's all I got. He said as soon as I had a Need-to-Know clearance through Washington on that program, he would be glad to give me a complete briefing."

"So we forget it. In a week, if I feel like my bones are melting or something, we'll bully Dan Griggs into that Need-to-Know buzzer and fly back out there. I wonder if it could be something to do with a new energy source? You remember that it didn't go off when the gas exploded. It went off later, after the heat built up more."

"Shut up Mark, and forget it. Rest."

"It might be some kind of a new rocket propellant that would jolt our rockets up to the speed of light."

"Don't hold your breath on that one, Mark."

He laughed and looked at his bandaged hands and then at the 9-foot surf-fishing pole and the spinning reel Joanna had bought for him. He couldn't wait to use them. Slowly he sank down into the too-soft mattress. Another mission? That he could wait for. Right now all he wanted was for the next three days to pass so he could begin living again—and so he could try for some croakers or opel eye or maybe a small bonito in the surf.

Dear Reader:

The Pinnacle Books editors strive to select and produce books that are exciting, entertaining and readable . . . no matter what the category. From time to time we will attempt to discover what you, the reader, think about a particular book or series.

Now that you've finished reading this volume in *The Penetrator* series, we'd like to find out what you liked, or didn't like, about this story. We'll share your opinions with the author and discuss them as we plan future books. This will result in books that you will find more to your liking. As in fine art and good cooking, a matter of taste is involved; and for you, of course, it is *your* taste that is most important to you. For Lionel Derrick and the Pinnacle editors, it is not the critics' reviews and publicity that have been most rewarding, it is the unending stream of readers' mail. Here is where we discover what readers like, what they *feel* about a story, and what they find memorable. So, do help us in becoming a little more knowledgeable in providing you with the kind of stories you like. Here's how . . .

WIN BOOKS . . . AND $200! Please fill out the following pages and mail them as indicated. Every week, for twelve weeks following publication, the editors will choose, at random, a reader's name from all the questionnaires received. The twelve lucky readers will receive $25 worth of paperbacks *and* become official entrants in our Pinnacle Books Reader Sweepstakes. The winner of this sweepstakes drawing will receive a Grand Prize of $200, the inclusion of his or her name in a forthcoming Pinnacle Book (as a special acknowledgment, possibly even as a character!), and several other local prizes to be announced to each initial winner. As a further inducement to send in your questionnaire *now,* we will also send the first 25 replies received a free book by return mail! Here's a chance to talk to the author and editors, voice your opinions, and win some great prizes, too!

READER SURVEY

NOTE: Please feel free to expand on any of these questions on a separate page, or to express yourself on any aspect of your thoughts on reading ... but do be sure to include this entire questionnaire with any such letters.

---

1. Are you glad you bought this book, and did it live up to your expectations?

2. What was it about this book that induced you to buy it?
   - (A. The title____) (B. The author's name____)
   - (C. A friend's recommendation____)
   - (D. The cover art____)
   - (E. The cover description____)
   - (F. Subject matter____) (G. Advertisement____)
   - (H. Heard author on TV or radio____)
   - (I. Read a previous book in this series____ ... which ones? ____)
   - (J. Bookstore display____)
   - (K. Other? ____

3. What is the book you read just before this one?

   And how would you rate it with this volume in *The Penetrator* series? ____

4. What is the very next book you plan to read?

   How did you decide on that? ____

5. Where did you buy this volume in *The Penetrator* series? ____

(Name and address of store, please):
_____
_____

6. Where do you buy the majority of your paperbacks? _____

7. What seems to be the major factor that persuades you to buy a certain book? _____
_____

8. How many books do you buy each month? ____
_____

9. Do you ever write letters to the author or publisher . . . and why? _____
_____

10. About how many hours a week do you spend reading books? ____ How many hours a week watching television? ____

11. What other spare-time activity do you enjoy most?
_____ For how many hours a week? ____

12. Which magazines do you read regularly? . . . in order of your preference _____,
_____, _____,
_____, _____

13. Of your favorite magazine, what is it that you like best about it? _____
_____

14. What is your favorite television show of the past year or so? _____

15. What is your favorite motion picture of the past year or so? _____

16. What is the most disappointing television show you've seen lately? _____

17. What is the most disappointing motion picture you've seen lately? _____

18. What is the most disappointing book you've read lately? _____

19. Are there authors that you like so well that you read *all* their books? _____
    Who are they? _____

20. And can you explain *why* you like their books so much? _____
    _____
    _____

21. Which particular books by these authors do you like best? _____
    _____

22. What do you think of the Combat Catalog? Good idea _____ Good information, but not necessary _____

23. Which of Mark Hardin's activities do you find most interesting? Fishing _____ Flying _____ Practice of Indian craft _____ Indian philosophy _____ The women in his life _____ Sports and Physical training _____

24. Would you be interested in reading more about Mark Hardin's Indian heritage? Yes _____ No _____

25. Which of these women, who have appeared in recent adventures, would you want to see more of? Angie Dillon _____ Angela Perez _____ Samantha Chase _____ What is your opinion of them? _____
    _____

26. Of all the recent books you've read, or films you've seen, are there any that you would compare in any way to *The Penetrator*? _____

27. With series books that you like, how often would you like to read them . . . (a) twice a year _____? (b) three times a year _____? (c) every other month _____? (d) every month _____? (e) other _____?

28. What is your favorite book character or series of all time? _____
And why? _____

29. Do you collect any paperback series? _____ Which ones? _____

30. What do you like *best* about *The Penetrator* series? _____

31. And what don't you like about it . . . if anything? _____

32. Have you read any books in *The Destroyer* series? _____ And what is your opinion of them? _____

33. Have you read any books in the Nick Carter *Killmaster* series? _____ Opinion? _____
_____

34. Have you read any books in *The Death Merchant* series? _____ Opinion? _____
_____

35. Have you read any books in *The Executioner* series? _____ Opinion? _____

36. Have you read any books in the *Edge* series? _____ Opinion? _____
_____

37. Have you read any books in *The Butcher* series? _____ Opinion? _____

38. Have you read any books in the *Louis L'Amour* western series? _____ Opinion? _____

39. Have you read any books in the *Travis McGee* series? _____ Opinion? _____

40. Have you read any books in the *Matt Helm* series? _____ Opinion? _____

41. Have you read any books in the *Carter Brown* mystery series? _____ Opinion? _____

42. Rank the following descriptions of *The Penetrator* series as you feel they are best defined:

	Excellent	*Okay*	*Poor*
A. A sense of reality	_____	_____	_____
B. Suspense	_____	_____	_____
C. Intrigue	_____	_____	_____
D. Sexuality	_____	_____	_____
E. Violence	_____	_____	_____
F. Romance	_____	_____	_____
G. History	_____	_____	_____
H. Characterization	_____	_____	_____
I. Scenes, events	_____	_____	_____
J. Pace, readability	_____	_____	_____
K. Dialogue	_____	_____	_____
L. Style	_____	_____	_____

43. What do you do with your paperbacks after you've read them? _____
   _____

44. Do you buy paperbacks in any of the following categories, and approximately how many do you buy in a year?

   A. Contemporary fiction _____
   B. Historical romance _____
   C. Family saga _____
   D. Romance (like Harlequin) _____
   E. Romantic suspense _____
   F. Gothic romance _____
   G. Occult novels _____
   H. War novels _____
   I. Action/adventure novels (like *this* book) _____
   J. "Bestsellers" _____
   K. Science fiction _____
   L. Mystery _____
   M. Westerns _____
   N. Nonfiction _____
   O. Biography _____
   P. How-To books _____
   Q. Other _____

45. And, lastly, some profile data on *you* the reader...

   A. Age: 12–16____ 17–20____ 21–30____
      31–40____ 41–50____ 51–60____
      61 or over____

   B. Occupation: _____

C. Education level; check last grade completed:
10 _____ 11 _____ 12 _____ Freshman _____
Sophomore _____ Junior _____ Senior _____
Graduate School _____, plus any specialized
schooling _____

D. Your average annual gross income:
Under $10,000_____ $10,000–$15,000_____
$15,000–$20,000_____ $20,000–$30,000_____
$30,000–$50,000_____ Above $50,000_____

E. Did you read a lot as a child? _____ Do you
recall your favorite childhood novel? _____
_____

F. Do you find yourself reading more or less
than you did five years ago? _____

G. Do you read hardcover books? _____ How
often? _____. If so, are they books that you
buy? _____ borrow? _____ or trade? _____ Or
other? _____

H. Does the imprint (Pinnacle, Avon, Bantam,
etc.) make any difference to you when considering a paperback purchase? _____

I. Have you ever bought paperbacks by mail
directly from the publisher? _____ And do you
like to buy books that way? _____

J. Would you be interested in buying paperbacks via a book club or subscription program? _____ And, in your opinion, what

would be the best reasons for doing so? _____
_____ . . . the problems in
doing so? _____

K. Is there something that you'd like to see writers or publishers do for you as a reader of paperbacks? _____
_____

L. Would you be interested in joining a *Penetrator* fan club? _____
_____

M. If so, which of the following items would interest you most:

	GREAT IDEA!	DEPENDS . . .	FORGET IT!
Monthly Newsletter			
Membership card			
Membership scroll (for framing)			
T-shirt			
Sweat shirt			
Windbreaker jacket			
Poster			
Decal			
Other ideas?			

(On those items above that you *do* like, indicate what you think a fair price would be.)

THANK YOU FOR TAKING THE TIME TO REPLY TO THIS, THE FIRST PUBLIC READER SURVEY IN PAPERBACK HISTORY!

NAME _____

ADDRESS _____

CITY _____ STATE ____ ZIP ____

PHONE _____

Please return this questionnaire to:

The Editors; Survey Dept. PS
Pinnacle Books, Inc.
2029 Century Park East
Los Angeles, CA 90067

Subject to all federal, state, and local restrictions; void where prohibited by law.